Lark in an Alien Sky

by

REBECCA STRATTON

Harlequin Books

TORONTO • LONDON • NEW YORK • AMSTERDAM
SYDNEY • HAMBURG • PARIS

Original hardcover edition published in 1979
by Mills & Boon Limited

ISBN 0-373-02274-3

Harlequin edition published July 1979

CHAPTER ONE

ON such a lovely day Corinne knew she should have been feeling happy and lighthearted, especially in view of the fact that she had received a letter from Gregori. Instead it was his letter that caused her to feel so troubled and unsure of herself.

It was five weeks since she had heard from him last, and for the first time she was ready to admit that, almost without realising it, she had begun to have doubts about the wisdom of the step she had taken—now when it was almost too late. Gregori had written to say that he would be arriving in London on the twenty-first to take her back to Greece with him as his affianced bride.

It was typical of Gregori, she realised, that he stated his intentions firmly without even mentioning the possibility of her having different ideas. It was true that she had no family ties in England, and there was no sound reason why she should not be married in his country as they had agreed, but she would like to have had the chance of changing her mind.

Corinne had loved his confident, almost dominating manner, and had accepted it as being part of his character without taking exception to it—until now. Only now did she find herself feeling vaguely resentful at the way he informed her of his intent without seeking her present opinion.

It seemed scarcely possible it was only two months ago that she and Gregori had met for the first time in Paris. Corinne had been on holiday, and wandering around an open-air art exhibition on her first day there. She had been having a little trouble making herself understood by a persistent young artist who spoke no English, but still managed to make his meaning quite clear, and Gregori had come to her aid. Speaking fluent French, he told the young man exactly where he got off and, too surprised to say anything, Corinne had accepted his intervention without ever letting him know that she had been more amused than fearful of her unknown admirer's approach.

She had been attracted to Gregori even in those first few moments, for he was a man that women were bound to notice. In the bright and noisy gaiety of the narrow street, among the artists and their would-be clients, she had told him her name, Corinne Thomas, and he had looked vaguely puzzled for a moment until she repeated it.

Their first laughter had been shared over his confusion. The fact that her two names together, as she had said them, sounded very much like the Greek word for lark. It had become a habit from then on for him to call her 'my lark' whenever he used an endearment, and he had used that endearment, and others in his own tongue, with increasing frequency during the next three weeks.

After that first meeting he had escorted her back to her hotel and taken her to dinner that evening, and from then on they had seen one another every evening as well as whatever time Gregori had free from business meetings. It had seemed inevitable that their companionship should lead to romance.

He was a serious man for the most part, though not

without a sense of humour, and quite a lot older than she was, but Corinne found him irresistible. He was so different from any man she had known before, and his attractions became more apparent on closer association. He was a new and exciting experience.

Brown-skinned, black-haired and dark-eyed, he had seemed to bring the passion and warmth of another world into her life, and aroused in Corinne such emotions and desires as she had never known before, which she thought of now with a slight sense of diffidence. It had been all too easy to fall in love with Gregori, and when he had asked her to marry him on the last night before she had to fly back to London, she had accepted without hesitation because it seemed the natural conclusion to those perfect weeks together.

She had felt quite sure that she could never love anyone else as she did that mature and stunningly attractive man. It was not until she received his latest letter that she felt a definite doubt. She had, she realised, gradually reached the conclusion that she and Gregori had experienced nothing more than a holiday romance, inspired by the romantic atmosphere of Paris, no matter how real it had seemed at the time.

Because Gregori, as head of his family's shipping and export business, had to return to Greece, and Corinne had to serve out her notice with the company that employed her as a secretary, parting on a temporary basis had been inevitable, but in the beginning she had had no doubt at all about committing herself. Only now when it was almost too late to go back did it occur to her how much of a stranger he still was, and she felt a sudden panic at the thought of his being there any moment now.

It was Robert's suggestion that she was acting much

too impulsively that had set her thinking along the lines she was now, she had to admit. But there was truth in his suggestion that she had jumped in at the deep end, as he put it, and if she was going to pull out she must do it now, when Gregori came for her.

He knew she was free of her commitments by now, he said, and that she would have made all the necessary arrangements to accompany him home to Greece. Such arrangements, she knew, he would not normally have left to a woman, but he knew her to be an efficient junior secretary; she had told him that herself.

He could not come sooner, she realised that, he was a very busy and important man, but she wished he had given her more than the two days he had. Given longer she could have sat down and written him a sensible and well considered letter, and explained how she felt. As it was he would be with her any moment now and she still was not ready for him. Nor would he be pleased about her changing his plans for their meeting.

But she chose the park because she could not be certain her flatmate would give them the privacy their meeting required, for Vanessa was inquisitive, tactless and quite often malicious. Corinne dared not risk trying to explain her present doubts to Gregori with the fear constantly on her mind that they might be interrupted. Here in a public park they could enjoy a curious kind of detachment while still surrounded by people, and the weather was warm and sunny.

She could visualise his black frown when he got the message with no time to reply or to change the venue again, and she tried to stop her hands from trembling as she sat on a bench under the trees and told herself she was doing it for both their sakes. Those five weeks seemed suddenly like a lifetime, and the ten minutes she had sat there even longer.

If only she could not so easily recall every detail of his features and the long easy stride as he came towards her, impatient for their reunion. The remembrance of that bright dark gaze confidently noting the responsive smile he knew would be there on her face when she saw him, and the touch of his mouth like a burning brand on her senses made her feel suddenly afraid. So much so that her stomach churned sickeningly, and she could not tell if it was sheer panic or the same kind of wild excitement he had always aroused in her.

It was a second or two before she realised that the familiarity of his face and that long-legged stride were no longer merely in her memory. Getting swiftly to her feet as he came towards her across the grass, she slid the tip of her tongue anxiously over dry lips and clasped her hands tightly together to stop them from trembling. She had anticipated his frown, and sure enough his black brows were drawn into a line above gleaming dark eyes that searched for some clue to her reason for changing his plans.

Lithe and sun-tanned, virile and sensual, but perfectly controlled until desire released a man of passion and gentleness; a lover who could sweep her to heights she had never dreamed of until she knew him. And it was against the memory of those times that she steeled herself as he came towards her.

'Corinne!'

He took her hands in his and Corinne's senses responded in an instant to the strong pressure of his fingers and the deep caressing warmth of his voice. He looked deep into her eyes so that she hastily averted them, her smile wavering.

'How are you?'

His manner was formal enough, but not his touch, and she took a second or two to bring her emotions under control before she answered him. 'I'm fine, thank you, Gregori. Are you?'

He nodded briefly, then turned and looked around at the sun-dappled paths and the people in their immediate vicinity, and his frown deepened. 'Where would you like to go?' he asked, and Corinne shook her head.

'Nowhere—I thought we could talk here.'

'Out here in the park?'

Obviously he did not understand her in this mood and Corinne felt a momentary twinge of conscience for making their meeting so public, but it was too late to do anything about it now. 'We can walk or sit down,' she told him, 'I don't mind which. It's very warm and I thought the sunshine and— -' She glanced at him uneasily. 'I suppose it isn't a very conventional place for what we have to talk about, but I thought—— Would you rather go somewhere else?'

He looked around once more, then shrugged his broad shoulders and sat down on the bench, pulling her down with him and still holding her hands. 'I do not understand,' he said, and there was an edge of steel on the normally velvet smooth voice. 'I understand nothing of this, Corinne. I ask that you be ready to leave with me and instead I find you sitting here in a public park, as if you have merely come out for an afternoon walk!'

'I can explain, Gregori—— '

'I hope that you can!' His stern air of authority was something new to her, although she had noticed it briefly when he dealt with that persistent young man in Paris, on their first meeting. 'Very obviously you are not ready to leave as I expected, and just as clearly you have something on your mind which I suspect you know I will not like! I do not understand any of it, Corinne, and I wish you would explain it to me.'

He had made no attempt to kiss her; though whether it was because he sensed something of what was in her mind or whether he felt a certain reticence after so long, she could not even guess. But it was because she did not want to see a look of hurt in his eyes when she told him her decision that she kept her own averted.

'I don't quite know how to begin,' she confessed in a breathless voice that must surely have given him an inkling of her predicament. But he neither encouraged nor discouraged her.

She eased her fingers free of his hold because she found the touch of him too disturbing and she needed to keep her wits about her if she was to be as firm as she must. It was so much more difficult than she had anticipated, and she was much too aware of him there beside her; he brought back too many memories. He was tall, she had forgotten just how tall, and he seemed to tower over her even sitting on the park bench, with his black head slightly bowed and waiting for the words she was finding so difficult to say.

'I—I want you to understand that—I've thought a lot about this and—— I'm sorry, Gregori. I'm sorry, but I just can't go on with it.' He said nothing and she wished he would. If he would berate her, lose his temper, anything but sit there while she struggled on, using her hands to make small, helpless gestures of appeal. 'I'm sorry, but I can't go through with the marriage!'

He reacted at last, taking possession of her hands once more in a grip so cruelly tight that she winced and caught her breath. 'So that is it!' That cutting edge was on his voice still and Corinne shrank from it. Until now she had never been the subject of his displeasure, only of his love, and she felt suddenly very small and uncertain. 'You are telling me that you have changed your mind, that it is all over, yes?'

He was going to make it even harder for her, and she felt so utterly miserable that it was hard to believe she was the one trying to make the break. 'I'm sorry.' She repeated the apology because there seemed so little else she could say at the moment, and Gregori made a short, sharp impatient sound as he squeezed her hands.

'You have such a short memory, Corinne!' The deep voice was relentless, scourging her with its scorn, and she shook her head in silent protest when he went on, 'Do you find it so easy to forget how you loved me? To forget those weeks in Paris when we were, or so I believed, the whole world to one another? I would have taken an oath that you loved me then—you fooled me very successfully!'

'Oh no, I *didn't*!' Her voice wavered uncertainly. 'It's just that—I'm no longer sure *how* I feel, Gregori, that's the trouble!'

He looked around the park at the people taking the sunshine and frowned more darkly than ever, as if he resented their proximity. 'So you chose a public park for our meeting, to make quite sure that I did not attempt to persuade you to change your mind, eh?'

'Oh, Gregori, please don't!'

She found his scorn the hardest thing of all to take and stirred uneasily. They sat close together and touching, like lovers, and yet they were a world apart at this moment and Corinne felt strangely lost. It was a reaction she did not attempt to understand and she shook her head in that vague, helpless way once more.

'I wasn't sure where to suggest,' she told him. 'I couldn't be sure that my flatmate wouldn't come barging in while you were there, and a place like this does have a kind of privacy because no one takes much notice of people in parks.' She glanced up briefly at his dark, frowning face. 'I seem to remember that you liked St James's Park when we came here on your last visit.'

From the way his eyes gleamed she thought he remembered the last occasion very well, and his hold on her hands tightened for a moment. 'Ah, so you do still have some feeling left for me, Corinne?' He caught her eye and for a moment she was caught up in the warm passionate glow of remembrance. 'You have not completely dismissed me from your life if you remember such little things!'

It was a point she had not considered and she hastily evaded his eyes once more as she made her explanation. 'I'm sorry, Gregori, I should have written to you and told you how I felt. It would have been much easier and saved us both a great deal of embarrassment. I just didn't think whèn I suggested you meet me here.'

Even to her own ears it sounded much too blunt and unfeeling, and not at all as she had meant it to be. She had not the slightest wish to hurt him or to be brutally frank, only to let him know that she at least had been brought back to earth by a return to ordinary everyday life. That an affair such as theirs had been could only live in the rarified atmosphere of Paris in the spring, and she was no longer so sure of either herself or of him.

But Gregori's eyes were exploring her face slowly, feature by feature, lingering on the full softness of her mouth that trembled uncertainly, and the sweep of brown lashes that shadowed her cheeks, and she felt her heart responding as it had always done before, to the promise in his eyes.

'And do you really believe that I can simply be put away with a few lines of written explanation?' he asked, his voice softened for a moment. 'After what we knew in

Paris, do you think I could be so easily dismissed, Corinne? Could you forget how I loved you then, my sweet lark? I have had no change of heart, I feel the same passion and desire for you that I felt when I asked you to become my wife. I still wish to make you my wife, it is for that reason I am here.'

Corinne stirred uneasily. Her fingers were cramped by his strong grip and she felt the kind of excitement making her blood leap that she had not known since their last meeting. Obviously he could still touch her senses and arouse in her, emotions that no other man ever had, and she sat for a moment trying to still the thudding beat of her heart while he watched her, his eyes steady and challenging between their thick lashes.

Yet she still hesitated; too unsure about committing herself to the role he had allotted her. The thought of flying off to Greece with him and becoming his bride filled her with a strange sense of alarm, and she knew that her hesitation angered him. It showed in the sudden, barely perceptible tightening of his mouth and the brighter gleam in his eyes as he looked down at her.

'The fact that I admit my desire for you does not touch you at all?' he asked, and she was tempted to tell him just how closely it touched her, but he gave her no time to say anything. Instead he let go her hands and turned himself round to sit straight-backed on the hard bench seat with his hands thrust into his pockets. 'I can see that it does not,' he declared. 'But if I cannot touch your heart, Corinne, consider the more practical side of the question. If you have no concern for my emotions, at least consider my pride!'

'Your pride?'

Briefly puzzled, Corinne frowned up at him, and he nodded his head firmly. 'You once told me that it was no small part of my character,' he reminded her with a touch of bitterness, and Corinne recalled the instance with a faintly rueful smile.

'You thought it amusing,' she remembered.

He no longer thought it amusing, it seemed, and he pressed on with his purpose relentlessly. 'Acting upon your promise and your attitude when I saw you last,' he said, 'I have announced to my family and friends that I am bringing home an English bride who loves me, and will make me a very able and suitable wife!'

'There was some opposition?' Corinne asked.

She felt pretty sure there had been, for something in his manner suggested it. Perhaps his family wished him to take a bride from his own people and disliked the idea of a foreign wife. If that was so it was not a thought to encourage her, but Gregori did not answer at once, instead he sat watching a group of children who were running along beside the low railing that surrounded the lake, and shouting at the ducks.

'*Was* there opposition, Gregori?'

He turned the steady gaze back to her and he had never before seemed so autocratic, so that she wondered at anyone having the temerity to challenge his choice. 'I choose my own wife,' he informed her, 'but in the circumstances you will understand that I am not of a mind to be jilted!'

It had not in fact occurred to Corinne that she was proposing to jilt him, and she caught her bottom lip between her teeth as she glanced at his face. His eyes were concealed for the moment, but she hastily looked away again before he raised them.

'I'm sorry.'

Obviously her repetitious apology annoyed him, for he was frowning. 'If you cannot give me some practical reason for your attitude,' he told her firmly, 'I shall assume that your extraordinary behaviour is attributable to premarital nerves, and insist our betrothal stands!'

Corinne was between indignation and apprehension and she sat twisting her hands together while she looked at him and frowned. 'You can't insist, if I refuse to marry you,' she told him, but wondered even as she said it whether it was less the truth than she believed.

Gregori looked at her steadily for a moment, and the familiar shivers of excitement ran through her body once more, weakening her sense of purpose and bringing back remembered kisses on cool moonlit boulevards. 'You think not?' he enquired.

For the moment there was no one else in their immediate vicinity, but Corinne wondered vaguely if he would have done what he did next, whether or not they were observed. Taking her hands, he pulled her to her feet and stepped back into the shelter of the neatly trimmed privet screen that housed the bench they had been sitting on.

Held tightly by those inescapable hands there was little she could have done to resist, and she trembled when the move brought her into contact with the hard tenseness of his body. He had taken her by surprise and she could all too easily recall the excitement of being in his arms. Looking down into her face, his eyes had the deep dark look she remembered so well; a look that seemed to strip her soul bare.

'Corinne?'

She was bound to react to that soft, enquiring use of her name, and she could not deny that he could still arouse her senses as no one else had ever done. But she had steeled herself to make the break, and she was still unconvinced that those halcyon days in Paris could be recaptured.

'Gregori——'. He was too close, and the lean, hard pressure of him was heart-stopping. 'I—I can see that you have cause to think I'm behaving badly——'

'Very badly, my lark!'

'But I'm doing it for both our sakes, I——'

Her mouth was effectively stopped, suddenly and breathtakingly, and the memories it stirred to life smothered for a moment her good intentions. Lifting her arms, she yielded her mouth to his and the softness of her body to the hard pressure of his arms. When he let her go she was already wavering and weakening, and his gleaming dark eyes suggested he knew it.

'Had you forgotten how it was, my lark?' he asked, and his voice was as soothing as the touch of silk.

Corinne swallowed hard and shook her head. All her instincts wanted her to say she would go with him after all, that she had been wrong to suppose anything had changed. But still a small voice of reason cautioned her, and she made conditions even as she yielded to her instincts.

'I'll go through with it,' she whispered. 'But——'

'There can be no buts, my love, I am leaving in a very short time and I wish to take you with me!'

'But I can't!' She avoided his eyes, tried to ignore the hands that pressed her close to him, and gave her mind to the practical aspects of the situation. 'I—you must allow me more time, Gregori. I came to meet you to tell you that it was finished, that I wouldn't come with you. I still think it's possible I'm making a mistake, but at least I'll agree to come out to Greece. You can send for me or come for me, but when I've had more time to get used to the idea. I can't just go dashing off with you today.'

His hands pressed her more firmly and she looked up into his face, at the fierce gleaming darkness of his eyes and the firm set of his mouth. 'That was not how you felt in Paris, Corinne,' he said in a deeply husky whisper that shivered with the passion she was all too familiar with. 'Then you would have come to the ends of the earth with me if I had asked it of you.' It was true, and Corinne's hastily lowered eyes confirmed it. His hands tightened and shook her lightly as he brought his face closer to hers. 'I do not like to be tossed this way and that by the fickleness of a woman, *kopéla mou*! Why can you not come as we arranged? You have resigned from your employment?'

Corinne nodded. She had done that in the first exciting days of anticipation, when she came back from Paris, and she had felt too embarrassed to ask for her job back again. For a week now she had been without a job and she needed to make up her mind exactly what she was going to do. Gregori, it seemed, had decided that for her.

'Then what is the problem?' he demanded.

She shrugged, shaking her head vaguely and wondering why, in the circumstances, she was being so obstructive. 'There are other things to consider before I go dashing off to Greece with you!'

Briefly his eyes narrowed and she thought she knew what he was thinking. 'Other things or other people?' he asked, and she was so certain he meant other men that she shook her head in denial.

'I have things to do before I leave. I haven't even packed, and that will take me quite a time.'

She shivered when his gaze swept down to her mouth

and lingered there, and she tried desperately to do something about the trembling weakness in her legs. Her heart
beat more wildly than ever when he pulled her closer and
she lifted her mouth to the warmth of his breath on her
lips. A light searching kiss coaxed them apart and she
saw it as inevitable when she lifted her arms and twined
them about his neck. Then he buried his mouth in hers
with the same burning ardour she could never forget, no
matter how long they were parted.

'Not too long, hmm?' he queried softly when he raised
his head for a moment, and Corinne shook her head.

The sun through the branches overhead was warmly
caressing, but she was conscious only of her own turbu-
lent desires and the fierce hard passion of his kiss.
Whether or not they were observed in the little arbour
behind the bench did not trouble her as she wound her
arms more tightly about his neck to bring him closer,
taking strength from his passion and responding with a
lack of inhibition that came to her only when she was
with him.

He released her mouth with lingering slowness and
it was as if someone had suddenly once more turned on
the birdsong and the sound of childish voices. 'I'll come
out to you,' she promised huskily, and despaired for a
moment of her original determination to be firm and
practical.

'Of course you will, my lark.' He smiled down at her
with such confidence that she knew he had never doubted
it. 'I never for one moment doubted that you would!'

His confidence amounted almost to arrogance and
aroused another reaction in her so that she looked up at
him with her chin angled and a gleam of warning in her
eyes. 'But not today,' she told him. 'I still have to pack,
for one thing.'

She felt him stiffen and the dark eyes narrowed once more. It was a moment or two before he replied and it occurred to Corinne as she waited for his reaction that quite possibly it was a new experience for Gregori Kolianos to meet resistance of any sort, either from the men he did business with or from women. His words, when he eventually did reply, were totally unexpected.

'I do not trust you, Corinne! You prevaricate still!'

For the moment she could not see that he had every reason to say what he did, and she was indignant at his lack of trust. 'But I've promised,' she told him. 'I shan't break a promise.'

Brown hands slid beneath the rich auburn cascade of her hair and rested on her neck, his thumbs gently stroking at the corners of her mouth, and his eyes glowed with promise as he told her, 'If you do, my lark, I shall come for you, make no mistake!'

A young woman wheeling a push-chair and keeping pace with a toddler glanced briefly in their direction, then quickly looked away again. But Corinne knew nothing but the firm insistent pressure of Gregori's kiss and the seductive caress of his hands.

As she quite often did at weekends, Corinne stayed with the Morgans. Although she was independent and shared a flat with another girl, it was almost like going home to go to the Morgans, for five years before, Ann and Clifford Morgan had taken her under their wing and seen her through the traumatic time after the death of both her parents in a car crash. They had known her parents, Clifford had gone to school with her father, and they had gladly come to her aid when she was left alone.

Robert was their only child and a couple of years older than she was, and he always treated her with a gentle consideration that was just what she needed in the first lonely months without her parents. He, far more than his parents, was against her going out to Greece and especially against her marrying Gregori. Now that it had come down to firmly making up her mind about it, Robert made no secret of the fact that he would influence her against it if he possibly could. His parents had said little, they allowed their son the privilege of making his own life and they conceded Corinne the same right, but it had become increasingly clear to her that they had hopes of her and Robert making a match, and that added to her discomfiture.

'It's an awful long way, dear,' Ann Morgan reminded her, her voice soft with the ghost of a Welsh accent, and Robert tutted impatiently, giving his opinion before Corinne could reply.

'It's the most crazy scheme I've ever heard!' he declared flatly. 'Going to a strange country to marry a man you scarcely know on the strength of a holiday romance! You must be mad!'

Ann gave her son a warning glance, but Corinne, remembering her own doubts, merely smiled ruefully at him and shook her head. 'I probably am,' she conceded, 'but I'm committed now, Robert, and I can't go back on my word.'

'I disagree,' Robert insisted firmly, his eyes bright with anger. 'With something as important as your whole future at stake, you're allowed to change your mind, even at the altar if need be!'

'I couldn't do that,' she said, but wondered if changing her mind at the altar, as Robert said, would make much difference. Gregori was not the man to let things go so far and then allow her to jilt him. 'I promised,' she added, and once more Robert left his opinion in no doubt.

'Then break the promise!' he said, but Corinne shook her head at him.

'It isn't as easy as you seem to think,' she told him. 'There's a lot involved, not least a certain amount of opposition from his family. Not that Gregori admitted it,' she added hastily, 'but I could tell from his manner. I know him well enough to tell that.'

She had added the last with a touch of defiance when she caught Robert's eye. 'You mean they've got someone lined up for him?' he asked. 'An arranged marriage?' He pursed his lips in a silent whistle. 'If that's how it is, Corinne, you're not going to be a very welcome alternative, are you?'

'I'm only guessing that's what was in his mind,' she told him. 'He's told his family and friends that he's bringing home an English bride and——'

'He doesn't want to lose face,' Robert suggested softly, and laughed in a way that brought a swift flush of colour to her cheeks. 'Oh, Corinne love, you can't marry a man just because he'll look a fool in front of his neighbours if you change your mind!'

'There's more to it than that,' she objected, and remembered then that Gregori had said he would come for her if she did not keep her promise and fly out to him very soon. 'You wouldn't understand, Robert, and—well, Gregori threatened that if I *don't* go to him, he'll be here to find out why.'

'*Will* he?' said Robert, his eyes gleaming. 'Well, let him come! I'll tell him you've had second thoughts and he can go off back to Greece and his family's choice of a bride, and forget about you! Not,' he added with a wry smile, 'that he'll find it easy to do; no man would. But he'll just have to put up with second best and marry his Greek lady!'

'Obviously he isn't in love with her,' Corinne said, and felt a curious sense of resentment at the idea of Gregori settling for second best with his Greek bride.

'And you can't possibly be in love with *him* after—how long is it?'

'It's a little over two months since we met,' Corinne replied, and he laughed shortly.

'There you are! And you've *known* him for barely more than three weeks out of that two months,' he reminded her, his mouth set firmly. 'You can't love him, Corinne, it just isn't possible!'

'It's possible,' Corinne argued confidently, and smiled across at Ann Morgan, seeking her support. 'Mama and Daddy were married when they'd known one another for only a few weeks, and they were wonderfully happy for more than twenty years. Mama never regretted being impulsive.'

'But they knew each other for quite a lot longer than you've known this—this Greek,' Robert insisted. 'Impulsive or not, she knew him for longer than three weeks before she married him!'

'She was so very much in love, I remember,' Ann Morgan recalled with a reminiscent smile, and her son frowned at her despairingly.

'But Corinne admits that isn't so in her case,' he reminded her.

'I thought I was, when I knew him in Paris,' Corinne mused, a small frown drawing her brows together as she recalled those cool spring evenings with Gregori. Long walks along the banks of the Seine with his arm about her and his voice close to her ear saying words in Greek that she did not always understand but could easily enough interpret from the warmth in his dark eyes. 'I very definitely was in love with him then and——' She shrugged uneasily, trying to shrug off ghosts of whispers and kisses and the magic of Paris. 'I don't know—I just wish I was more certain.'

'It was the atmosphere of Paris, dear,' Ann Morgan told her, giving substance to her own thoughts. 'It's such a very romantic place; I remember Clifford and I went there once and it had a kind of magic.'

'That's just my point,' Robert intervened swiftly. 'There's a special feeling about Paris, it's well known. You just let it go to your head, Corinne, you weren't serious, just—influenced.'

'At the time I was serious,' Corinne told him, 'and so was Gregori. He still is; I wish I knew for certain whether I am or not.'

'You'd better make haste and decide,' Robert said with a touch of asperity. 'You haven't got long to make up your mind!'

Robert had brought her to the airport, but he was reluctant to let her go, even now. He held both her hands and his eyes had a bright gleaming look that made her distinctly uneasy. 'Corinne!'

She glanced over her shoulder at the glass doors leading into the terminal building. 'I'd better go, Robert, I haven't much time if I'm to be there half an hour before take-off, as they say. It was nice of you to bring me, much better than having a taxi, though I'm glad your folks didn't come or I might have cried.'

'I brought you because I hoped all the way here that you'd say to turn round and take you back home,' he told her. 'I would never have so willingly wasted a journey as I would this one, and you must know it.' He too glanced at the glass doors as they slid open automatically to admit another passenger. 'It still isn't too late, Corinne.'

'No, Robert!'

She would have freed her hands, but he held them too tightly and when she turned he did too, walking with her through the departure lounge without once taking his eyes off her face. It was fairly quiet, although there were people going to and fro, and no one had time to notice them standing there with Robert's hands holding hers, as he brought them to a standstill again.

'I love you, Corinne.' She looked up at him swiftly, her eyes wide and, for the moment, slightly stunned. 'I always have,' he went on, speaking quietly but with a nervous urgency that was oddly affecting in the circumstances. 'I want you to stay and marry *me*, Corinne! I love you and always have!'

It was so ironic that Corinne almost laughed aloud. How different it might have been if only he had made his declaration earlier. 'Why didn't you say so before?' she asked with a hint of bitterness, and he frowned briefly as if it was not the answer he expected.

'Would it have made any difference to the way things are?'

She shook her head and gently freed her hands from his, looking across the wide, chillingly modern reception area when a distorted voice crackled from the broadcast system something about the flight for Athens. 'I wouldn't have been in a position to fall in love with Gregori if I'd been committed to you, would I?' she asked. 'I wouldn't have seen him again after that first time, nor would I have had the opportunity to know him as I did, or——' The voice crackled once more and she shook her head. 'It's too late now, Robert, and I have to go.'

He reached for her hands again and drew her close for a moment while he kissed her lips, then looked down into her face with the glow of desperation in his eyes. 'If you can say that, you surely know now that you don't really love him,' he insisted, but Corinne drew away quickly and turned to go.

'I loved him,' she said with a catch in her voice. 'I've yet to find out whether I still do or not. Goodbye, Robert, and—thank you for everything!'

'Corinne!'

She did not turn but waved a hand as she went, hurrying to answer the metallic summons of the flight call. The plane was waiting and somewhere only a few hours away Gregori would be waiting for her. She knew him well enough to know that he would be anxious, watchful, not yet sure that she would come as she had promised, and she did not see how she could have done other than fly out to him when he had so much at stake. His pride, as he had reminded her, was a considerable part of his character, and she still felt enough for him not to hurt him if she could help it.

CHAPTER TWO

It was like a great relief map spread out below when Corinne caught her first sight of Greece, and then gradually the details became more clear, the colours more definite. She felt a tingling glow of pleasure as well as excitement when she looked down on it, much as Zeus might have looked upon it from Mount Olympus.

The deep sapphire ocean was shredded by a wildly undulating coastline and scattered with a thousand tiny islands, as if someone had carelessly spilled a casket of jewels and left them to lie in the relentless sun. Delphi, Sparta, Olympia; all the magical names from the glorious days when the gods walked the earth were down there. The ruined temples and palaces of the fallen gods still standing on the same sunlit, wooded hillsides they had occupied when Aphrodite, the goddess of love, rose naked from the sea, and Apollo battled with the monster Python.

The sky had a gem-like blueness that was reflected in the sea and gave breathtaking violet hues to the crown of Mount Hymettus. An impression of dazzling whiteness became the contours of definable buildings as the plane dropped lower, and the sense of godlike remoteness receded before the practical normality of airport buildings and runways.

Down to earth once more, Corinne took a firm hold on her diminishing courage and followed her fellow passengers through the inevitable formalities. Smiling wryly to herself as she was passed through Customs, she wondered if any modern bride had come to her groom with quite so many doubts as she came to Gregori. Right up until the moment the aircraft landed she had been asking herself whether she had not been foolish to keep her promise to him, and yet the moment she saw him standing there waiting for her she felt such a sense of relief that she smiled instinctively.

Yet again it struck her what a striking man he was, and it gave her a curious and unexpected feeling of pride that he should be there to meet her and no one else. The moment she set eyes on him she put down her baggage and let him come to her, her heart hammering wildly as he came striding through the crowded hall.

He took her in his arms without hesitation and held her tightly with his face buried in her hair while he murmured words in her ear in his own tongue. Without her knowing their exact meaning, they nevertheless sent little shivers of pleasure through her, reminding her of other places, other times. He held her for some time like that, then looked down into her face with a hint of unmistakable challenge in his eyes.

'So,' he said, speaking English for the first time, 'you came!'

'I came,' Corinne agreed, and caught her breath anew when she was once more crushed in his arms.

Then he eased her away, just far enough that he could look into her eyes. He said nothing, but sought her mouth after a second or two and kissed her in a way that was guaranteed to make her unsteady legs even less capable of supporting her, and she clung to him from the sheer need of something to cling to. Beneath her hands the softness of his shirt pulsed with an urgently beating heart that almost matched her own, and it was as if she had never had doubts at all.

The sudden metallic sound of the announcer brought her back to a realisation of where she was, and curiously enough reminded her of Robert's much less affecting kiss, pressed on her in the few moments before she left him. With a hand on his chest, she pushed Gregori away and glanced up at his face for a second, once more plagued by uncertainty and doing her best to conceal it.

To people around them with time to speculate, they must have looked like a couple of lovers reunited, and she supposed they were in a way; certainly Gregori would have agreed with it. They had been lovers in Paris and as far as he was concerned they still were; it was only her own feelings that were in doubt, and the doubt must soon be resolved. For unless she had misjudged him, Gregori was not likely to be a patient bridegroom.

His hands were on her shoulders and his strong fingers curving into her flesh while he regarded her with gleaming dark eyes. 'I am so happy to see you, my lark!' The deep and unforgettable voice still had the same magical effect on her senses, and she smiled without being fully aware that she did. 'I am also relieved,' he went on with a touch of dryness, 'for I had fears right up until the moment I saw you that you would not keep your word to me. Yes, I confess to being fearful,' he added, as if by making such an admission he surprised himself.

It was on the tip of Corinne's tongue to let him know just how close she had come to confirming his fears, but she was here, on alien ground, and she felt a need for him that she could not deny. 'I made you a promise,' she reminded him, 'and I don't break promises without a very good reason.'

The brief glance he gave her seemed to doubt the truth of it, but he said nothing for the moment, and instead turned her in the direction of one of the exits, holding her arm in a firmly possessive grip that was oddly comforting. Looking up at him as they walked close together, her eyes had a hint of speculation.

'You said if I didn't come, you'd come over and fetch me,' she reminded him. 'Would you really have gone to so much trouble, Gregori?'

Her arm was crushed against him and he eyed her slightly flushed face for a moment before he answered her. 'Do you doubt it?' he asked, and when she grimaced doubtfully and shrugged, he paused in his step and bent to kiss her mouth hard. 'Never doubt it,' he told her huskily, and squeezed the arm he held. 'I do not easily let go that which I have made my own, you will learn that about me as you will learn many other things, my lark!'

However softly the words were spoken, there was something about the way he said them that aroused her to protest. His possessiveness and his determination to make her his own had thrilled her in the early days, but now that it was all too close to becoming a fact, she shied away from it.

'I don't *belong* to anyone, Gregori! I'm not a possession, like your house or your business!' It angered her to realise that he was treating her protest as if it was a mere gesture against the inevitable, and she frowned at him discouragingly. 'I mean it, Gregori—I'm not a possession!'

'I have not said that you are,' he denied, but a glance at his face revealed a glittering darkness in his eyes and his mouth had a disconcerting half-smile at its corners.

'I just want you to——'

'I want you to love my country,' he interrupted quietly, and once more bent his head to kiss her mouth. 'Welcome to Greece, *ágapitikóz*!'

Outside in the hot sunshine Corinne looked around her at the white buildings she had seen from the aircraft. Like all such views it was slightly less idyllic at ground level, but it was still exciting, and with Gregori's hand guiding her to where his car was parked, she had a sense of anticipation that was not all unpleasant.

Gregori settled her with solicitous care into the front passenger seat, then stood for a moment before he closed the door, looking down into her face with disconcerting steadiness. She was hot and flushed and she kept her eyes lowered because she found him much too disturbing.

Then he slid a hand beneath her chin and lifted it, leaning down to press his mouth over hers—a kiss that searched determinedly for a response from her. But Corinne could only think that she was on her way to his home, on her way to meet the family she believed to be firmly against her marrying Gregori, and her lips remained coolly unresponsive.

For a moment the glittering darkness of his eyes searched her face for a reason. 'You will be tired after the flight,' he decided, 'but the drive will give you time to rest a little before you meet my family.' He came around and got into the seat beside her but still did not start the engine; instead he half-turned to look at her. 'Is there something troubling you, Corinne?' he asked, and when she did not immediately answer him he frowned impatiently. 'If you tell me, I can put your mind at ease. Are you worried about meeting my family, is that it?'

How could she bluntly inform him that the very idea of meeting his family filled her with dread? She was tempted, but instead she told him a half-truth, making an excuse that would explain her reluctance without being too frankly provocative.

'I'm just nervous, Gregori. It's natural reaction in the circumstances.'

The pressure of his hand sought to reassure her, and did to some extent. 'I do not like you to be nervous of meeting my family,' he said. 'But of course it is natural, as you say, in the circumstances.'

'Just as it's natural that they're going to resent me!'

'No!' She had not meant to let him know what she expected, and clearly he disliked her mentioning it. 'No, Corinne!'

'But it's true, I know it is,' Corinne insisted. 'I know they don't really approve of you marrying me. Oh, I know you haven't said as much, but I can read between the lines! I assume they had someone—someone much more suitable that they'd rather you married. A Greek girl who would be a credit to the Kolianos name and not a junior secretary from a foreign country who——'

'Corinne, stop it!' His sharp admonishment brought her up short and for a moment she looked vaguely ashamed of her moment of self-pity.

'I'm sorry,' she murmured, 'but I can't help feeling that before long I'm going to regret this trip even more than I do now.' She considered for a second, then glanced at him from the corners of her eyes. 'You *would* have married someone else, a Greek girl, if I had decided not to come after all, wouldn't you?' she challenged, but caught her breath at his answer.

'Almost certainly,' he said. I am the only surviving son and as such I have a responsibility to provide the next generation.' He caught her look and narrowed his eyes. 'Does that shock you?' he asked, and Corinne shook her head dazedly.

She had to admit, when she looked at him, that she would have found it difficult to take if Gregori had simply accepted her initial decision to end it between them, and not been so insistent that she keep her promise to marry him. If he had come home and taken the Greek bride that she felt sure his family had in mind for him, as he had declared he would. It was a dog-in-the-manger attitude perhaps, but one she did not attempt to excuse at the moment.

Gregori stroked a long forefinger down her cheek, and there was a hint of a smile on his mouth as he studied her for a moment. 'Is it not fortunate for me that I was able to find someone whom I could love, before my mother despaired of making a husband of me?' he asked, and leaned forward to kiss her mouth.

Just for a moment Corinne felt the same wild abandon she had known first in Paris, and she yielded to the irresistible excitement of it. Only when he released her mouth with lingering slowness and she looked up into the dark, passionate face did she remind herself that he was still such an unknown quantity to her. He was a stunningly exciting stranger, but a stranger nevertheless, and she could not lose sight of the fact.

Stroking his big hands over the soft curve of her cheeks, he studied her with gleaming dark eyes. 'Now I will take you home, my love,' he said.

It was impossible not to be excited by her first acquaintance with Greece, and Corinne found it quite enough to take her mind, at least momentarily, off the situation that lay ahead of her. Rather disconcertingly Athens proved to be a thriving modern city, although she had only to raise her eyes to see the Acropolis outlined against a sky just as incredibly blue as any picture postcard. It was much more immediate than all the pictures she had seen, dangled like irresistible bait before would-be travellers tired of the modern world.

There were suburban houses and factories, modern shops and a polyglot collection of people who could have belonged anywhere in the world. It was only glimpses of ancient glories, never very far away and tangled inextricably with modern development, that proclaimed the difference between Greece and any other country, and made it the cultural Mecca of half the world.

Once beyond Athens itself, the scene began to change, though only slowly. The coast road led them through Glyfáda with its wonderful beaches, past villas and exclusive hotels set amid pine trees and rocks. Through Voula where the foothills of Hymettus met the sea, the gentle slopes covered with bushes of wild thyme and origan and reminding Corinne that the bees there still provided what was claimed to be the best honey in the world; the nectar of the gods.

Pine-clad promontories formed charming little bays with sandy beaches and warm red rock, and living there could be idyllic, she thought. It did not yet occur to her that it was to just such an idyll that Gregori was taking her.

It was a moment or two before she detected a certain air of tension about him, and glanced at him curiously. He kept his eyes on the road they were following, but every so often he would send a swift glance to their left, as if he was watching for something, and following his glance she knew suddenly that her journey was almost at an end.

Among a cluster of tall pine trees just ahead she caught sight of a gleaming white building, and guessed that Gregori was home. So sure was she that her heart began to beat harder and faster as tantalising glimpses of the building danced between the crowding pines like sunlight on water.

Gregori turned the car into a narrow, pine-shadowed road that wound upward as well as round, and gave her a brief look over his shoulder as they began to climb. 'Soon now,' he promised, and there was something about the way he said it that suggested he too might have certain reservations about the coming meeting with his family.

Corinne simply nodded, for it was too late for words. The situation had snowballed beyond recall and soon she would know exactly how Gregori's family felt about his marriage to a foreign girl, some years his junior and as poor as a church mouse by their standards.

While the car wound its way along the narrow road through the pines she thought about Robert and how earnestly he had sought to dissuade her from this trip. She was still not quite sure why she had been so insistent about keeping her promise to Gregori, and as she looked at the dark sternness of his profile against a background of pine trees, she wondered if she would ever be completely sure of anything concerning him.

His gentleness seduced her, but his arrogance sometimes made her bristle with resentment. She was too uncertain about spending the rest of her life with him to feel pleasure at the prospect of being his wife, and yet she could not bear to think of him marrying anyone else. She had never felt so confused as she did at this moment, and it was much too late to turn back now.

The house seemed to materialise with miraculous suddenness and stood before them, large and white, glistening in the sunlight and heart-stoppingly impressive. It had been built in a clearing, but the clearing had been transformed into magnificent gardens that were a mass of colour and scent. The effect of coming upon it so suddenly was breathtaking, and her instinctive gasp of pleasure made Gregori turn his head and smile.

'It surprises you?'

'Yes, I suppose it does,' Corinne admitted without quite knowing why it should.

Heaven knew what she had expected, but certainly not this paradise of beauty and colour that surrounded them as the car swept around a bed of red roses to stop in front of the house. Wide borders edged the open space in front of the house and continued on out of sight at either side of it, richly overflowing with oleanders, hibiscus, roses and carnations and a dozen other species that Corinne did not attempt to identify.

Close to the house too the pine trees gave way to more exotic types, and figs, oranges and eucalyptus shaded the house and softened and muted its dazzling whiteness with fluttering patterns. The variety of different scents was almost overpowering as she stepped out of the car, and she breathed deeply at the headinness of them while Gregori's steadying hand lent his assistance.

Three steps led upward from the driveway and at first sight Corinne almost imagined that he had brought her to some ancient temple. Double doors stood partly open and showed a glimpse of cool whiteness and a ceiling that soared into shadows, and with a flutter of dismay she recognised that it was simply the entrance hall to his home.

Taking her arm, he took her up the steps and into the house, then turned and looked at her enquiringly. She knew what he was asking her with that silent glance, and she nodded automatically, doubting if he really knew just how much of an ordeal this introduction was going to be for her. She had not expected him to live in a shepherd's cottage, but this great house with its air of voluptuous luxury was equally unexpected, and she stared around her in the few moments before anyone else appeared.

The ceiling was smooth and pure white, while the walls were cut into a series of small niches along two sides, the smoothly curved edges surrounded by a gilded relief of leaves. The floor was tiled in a mosaic of muted reds and blues with gilt surrounds and a tall plant of some kind occupied a squat white urn at the foot of a curving staircase.

That much Corinne had time to see before a door opened and they were no longer alone. A girl about her own age came towards them, tall and angular, with black hair and gleaming dark eyes that made no secret of her curiosity. Head thrown back, she greeted Gregori with a few abrupt words in Greek, then looked very deliberately at Corinne with a smile on her bright red mouth.

'This is Corinne, my fiancée,' Gregori said, ignoring whatever it was she had said to him in Greek. 'Corinne, *ágapitikóz*, this is my sister Zoe. You are the same age and I am sure you will become good friends.'

Put as Gregori put it there was little doubt that he had made his wishes known to them both and that he expected them to comply. For her part Corinne was ready to make friends with anyone in the circumstances, and not simply to oblige Gregori, so she extended a hand unhesitatingly. Zoe Kolianos enclosed her hand with long slim fingers and her dark eyes still took stock of her quite openly as she did so. Quite obviously curiosity was her reason for being there.

'*Kalispéra sas, thespinís*,' she said in a light cool voice, and Gregori frowned.

Quite clearly it was not the welcome he had expected from his sister, and Corinne, with a sinking feeling in her stomach, suspected that she had just received her first snub from the Kolianos family. It was not an encouraging start, and as if he realised how she felt Gregori took her arm once more and drew her with him across the hall, leaving his sister standing there and watching them with dark resentful eyes.

They made for the room that Zoe had just left, but in the same moment that Gregori reached for the handle the door was opened and another woman stood framed in the doorway. She was older than Zoe, more Gregori's age and, Corinne was thankful to notice, much less obviously unwelcoming.

She had gentle dark eyes that switched quickly from Gregori to Corinne and back again before she stepped back to let them into the room, smiling as Gregori turned to introduce her. 'We thought we heard you arriving,' she told him, and her use of English instead of her native Greek gave Corinne yet another reason to hope that this woman, whoever she was, might prove to be an ally.

Even Gregori's grip on Corinne's arm seemed to have eased a little while he introduced them, as if the woman's greeting and made him feel a little less tense. 'Irine, *ágapiménoz*,' he said, 'I would like you to meet Corinne, my fiancée. Irine Kolianos, my sister-in-law.'

Quite obviously he was fond of her and on impulse Corinne decided that she too could become fond of Irine Kolianos in time. Her smile had a certain reserve, but it was not unfriendly, and she did not cut short her handshake as Zoe had done. 'I am most pleased to meet you, Miss Thomas, welcome to Greece.' Her pronunciation of Corinne's second name was not quite right, but then Gregori had not used it when he introduced her. Possibly she had used the formality of the second name because she wished first to make sure a more familiar approach was welcome.

'Mitéra is waiting,' she told Gregori, and led the way across the room. 'We had thought the flight was late, perhaps.'

No one either confirmed or denied it, but Corinne felt her legs again threatening to let her down as she approached an elderly woman who sat tall and straight in one of the armchairs. Given a choice she would have preferred to take refuge in whatever accommodation had been prepared for her until she could recover something of her normal self-confidence, but apparently Gregori wanted to introduce her to his family without delay.

The room itself was almost spartan in its simplicity, but at the same time bore the unmistakable stamp of comfort and luxury. The leather armchairs looked deep and comfortable and her feet sank into the deep pile of an Indian carpet, while pale walls, coloured a shade somewhere between cream and the palest grey, reflected the evening sunshine on water from somewhere outside.

Corinne knew something about Madame Argori Kolianos, for Gregori had occasionally mentioned her during their affair in Paris. He had spoken of her with a kind of critical affection, for apparently he gave her cause for doubt sometimes, despite his skilful handling of their company's affairs.

Her elder son, on whom she had pinned all her hopes for the future of Kolianos and Company, had died a year or two before his father did and it was Gregori who inherited the enormous responsibility of the vast shipping business. Not that she disliked her younger son, for he had been the apple of her eye, but she did not see him as a business man and she had never quite learned to trust the family fortunes to him.

Seeing the woman who now waited to be introduced to her, Corinne could understand something of the awe that Gregori claimed she was held in by the rest of the family. She was about sixty-three or four years old and handsome without any pretence at prettiness. Quite clearly it was from his mother that Gregori had inherited his arrogant self-assurance, for she looked the epitome of matriarchy as she sat watching them steadily from across the room.

Her hair was streaked with grey and her angular face lined and grave, her eyes unsmiling but not incurious. She gave her son a look of unmistakable impatience because he had stopped to introduce Corinne to his sister-in-law before bringing her across to her.

'Mama, may I introduce Corinne Thomas, my fiancée.'

A beringed hand was proffered unhesitatingly and Corinne only just managed to suppress a wince of pain when the rings on her fingers pressed into her flesh with the firmness of the grip. 'Corinne; my mother, Madame Argori Kolianos.'

'You are welcome to Greece, Miss Thomas.' The strong voice was heavily accented but perfectly intelligible, and despite the lack of a smile, Corinne felt that there was a certain amount of sincerity in the greeting. She welcomed her to Greece, though not necessarily to her home. 'You have not been to our country before?'

'No, Madame Kolianos, this is my first time.'

Madame Kolianos nodded, her mouth firmly set below an autocratic nose. 'Ah, then you will have much to learn of our ways, eh, *kopéla*?' She looked at her son once more but her expression did not change. 'Let us hope that my son proves to be a good instructor!'

If Gregori read anything significant into the adjoinder he gave no sign of it, but took her along to where the only other occupant of the room sat watching them with frankly curious eyes. She was about sixteen or seventeen years old and had something of the same look of defiant challenge that Zoe Kolianos had, but she got to her feet when they approached. More, Corinne suspected, because her upbringing had taught her courtesy rather than for any other reason.

'And this is Iole,' said Gregori, and stroked a light hand down the girl's flushed cheek. 'Iole is Irine and my brother Dimitri's child.'

'I am not a child, Thíos Gregori!'

Her reproach was swift and indignant and Corinne noted how good her English was, noticing that even at a moment like this she used the alien tongue out of courtesy. But Corinne could sympathise with her, for at seventeen it was belittling to be referred to as a child, especially if it was taken literally.

Gregori had never struck her as malicious and she wondered at his lack of tact in this instance, but here in his own home he was subtly different from the man she had known in Paris. This was his home ground and it was fairly obvious from what she had seen so far that he held the whip-hand in his capacity as head of the family.

It seemed for a second or two as if he might ignore his niece's reproach, but then he laughed shortly and kissed the girl's cheek. 'Iole is just seventeen,' he told Corinne, 'and she feels the need to spread her wings. Never mind, little one,' he added, and stroked the soft flushed cheek with a forefinger, 'you will soon learn to trim your wings and accept the word of those who are older and wiser than you are.'

Corinne had been about to step in, albeit very cautiously, and suggest that at seventeen it was natural to spread one's wings a little, when Iole spoke up on her own behalf, her eyes bright with defiance. 'Why must I trim *my* wings, Thíos Gregori?' she demanded. 'You do not trim *yours*; you do as you please and choose where you will, no matter who——'

'Iole!'

A little thrill of warning ran along Corinne's spine as Irine Kolianos called her daughter to order and came across the room to her. The gentle face looked vaguely anxious, but Gregori was already dismissing the reprimand she had been about to deliver, and he gave his attention to his niece once more. Iole's rash words had been enough to confirm all Corinne's worst fears and he was, she suspected, intent on subduing that small rebel with all the force of his powerful personality.

'You speak without thought, little one,' he told her

with such gentleness that it did not immediately strike Corinne just how iron-hard the hand was in the velvet glove. 'I am a great deal older than you are and see things more clearly. When you have lived for almost thirty-six years then you will have a better understanding of matters that seem to you so simple now.'

But Iole's dark eyes had a bruised and hurt look and she still blamed him, no matter how gently he sought to persuade her. To Corinne who knew nothing of what lay behind this exchange, it seemed that Gregori was trying to impress his will on the girl regarding something she felt strongly about, and she sympathised with her instinctively.

'If I live to be twice thirty-six years,' Iole told her uncle defiantly, 'even if you marry me to Costas Menelus tomorrow, I shall still feel the same way about——'

'Iole!'

Her grandparent's voice reminded her that there was a stranger in their midst and for a moment Iole's dark eyes rested on Corinne, as if she weighed her chances of getting sympathy from the newcomer. But Madame Kolianos extended a hand to her encouragingly, and after a moment or two Iole responded to the summons.

'*Éla, pethí,*' her grandmother soothed, and kissed her as she drew her into the curve of her arm.

To Corinne the sudden eruption of a family quarrel had momentarily taken her mind off her own position, but she felt she could not long remain aloof from whatever it was they felt so deeply about if it concerned marrying off a seventeen-year-old girl against her will. That was barbaric and she could not stand by and let it happen; but first she must know more about it.

'I am sorry, Corinne.' She brought herself swiftly back to earth and smiled automatically at Gregori, although she noted the tight line of his mouth and the glittering darkness of his eyes with a certain misgiving. 'We should not greet you with our private disagreements, it is most inhospitable.' He took her hand and squeezed her fingers lightly. 'You must be feeling tired too, my love, and in need of a bath, eh?'

'It would be nice,' Corinne admitted without hesitation, and he bent his head to kiss her beside her ear.

'Take all the time you need,' he whispered. 'Irine will show you to your room and if you feel hungry before it is time for dinner you must have something to eat—we do not dine until nine o'clock.'

'I can survive until then.' She smiled as she brushed back thick auburn strands from her forehead. 'But I'd love a bath and a few minutes to get my breath back, if Madame Kolianos will be so kind as to show me where my room is.'

Corinne realised her mistake too late, and the older woman's voice cut short Irine's attempt to answer. 'My daughter-in-law is known as Kiría Kolianos to those outside the family, Miss Thomas,' she informed Corinne, 'or as Irine to her family. The title Madame Kolianos carries a—certain honorary meaning in my case.'

'I'm sorry, *madame*.'

Corinne's cheeks coloured furiously, not only because of the reprimand but in anger at her own foolishness in forgetting for a moment what Gregori had told her. Obviously she was meant to see herself as outside the family privileges, but Gregori was speaking up, making *his* opinion clear before there were any more misunderstandings.

'There is no need for confusion,' he said in a firm confident tone, 'nor is there need for titles except in Mama's case, naturally. As my fiancée you will of course call us all by our first names, Corinne, and we in turn will call you Corinne. All of us,' he emphasised, giving Madame Kolianos a long hard look which his mother chose to ignore for the moment.

Corinne said nothing, she merely stood beside him and tried to subdue the sudden urge she felt to leave that big handsome room and never come back. The present situation, about how she should be treated, was something she suspected was likely to happen again in the future, and for a moment she wished herself back in the cosy familiarity of the Morgans' little sitting-room.

Even the flat, with Vanessa's constant comings and goings, would have seemed welcoming after this luxurious room with its atmosphere of antagonism. It was when Irine Kolianos turned and smiled at her encouragingly that she realised that Gregori's sister-in-law was likely to be the one to whom she turned most often. Irine was the one to smooth her way in this house of proud and arrogant people.

'Will you come with me?' she asked, and thankfully Corinne nodded.

'Gladly,' she said, and meant it.

They walked in silence across the vast hall as far as the staircase, and then Irine Kolianos turned once more and smiled at her. 'It is all very strange,' she suggested in that gentle voice of hers, and Corinne nodded agreement. A light hand was pressed for a moment on to her arm. 'I know how it feels,' Irine assured her. 'I too was a nervous bride. I came here first as Dimitri's betrothed and I was so afraid of them all that I could scarcely stand, but I learned to love them all, as you will.'

'More to the point,' Corinne suggested as they climbed the wide staircase together, 'is whether they'll ever take to me.'

Irine smiled and nodded assurance, but to Corinne their situations were not comparable. Irine would no doubt have come as Dimitri's bride with the full approval of his family, but with Corinne it was different.

She was not only from a different country and obviously not the woman whom Madame Kolianos would have chosen for her only surviving son's wife, but she brought no dowry with her, no wealth to swell the already rich coffers of the Kolianos fortunes. What was more it was not even absolutely certain that she would marry Gregori, even though she had flown out here to him. No, there could be no comparison with Irine's case —with her and Gregori it was quite different.

CHAPTER THREE

CORINNE soon found that shopping in Athens with Irine was a lot different from shopping at home; for one thing she had never in her life before had so much money to spend and the thought of such lavishness both delighted and alarmed her. It was something she must get used to, she supposed, but the idea of having a wedding gown specially designed and created for her alone was a breathtaking experience. Gossamer lace and whispering silk gave her a thrill of pleasure, and she could not help feeling excited by the prospect of wearing the creation that the designer promised.

Then too, there were day dresses and evening dresses. Hand-painted silks in exquisite colours shimmered like

expensive rainbows through her fingers as she dazedly
tried to choose one or two from so many. Irine whirled
her round so many shops looking at jewellery, lingerie
and furs that she sank gratefully on to a hard chair in
the café where they eventually took a break for coffee.

For a moment while they sat there amid the chatter
and the delicious smells of coffee and pastries, Corinne
thought about how different her wedding might have
been. Suppose Robert had professed his love for her
earlier, would she have married him? she wondered. She
was not at all sure that she would, for although she was
admittedly fond of him, she had never thought of him
in any other way but as a brother or a cousin—not until
that that day at the airport.

'You are dreaming about your wedding day?'

Irine's voice broke into her thoughts and she looked
across at her and smiled. If only Irine knew it, she was
the mainstay of her existence in her uncertainty, and she
often wished that it was Irine and not Zoe who was
Gregori's sister. Zoe, who was so abrasive and determinedly unfriendly that she must surely have some reason
for being as she was, other than simply personal dislike.

Irine was so obviously enjoying all the preparations
for the wedding that it would have been heartless to do
other than share her enjoyment, even though it was only
a token gesture most of the time. 'I was thinking of what
a riot of spending we've indulged in this morning,' she
laughed. 'I'd never have dared to spend so much on my
own, Irine.'

'You have enjoyed yourself?' Irine asked, and she
nodded. 'Then it is worthwhile!' she declared. 'Gregori
would expect you to buy whatever you need——'

'Want would be a more apt word!' Corinne told her.
'I'm being thoroughly spoiled and I know it!'

'And why should he not spoil you?' Irine wanted to know. 'It is the first time he has loved a woman enough to want to marry her, and the fact that she is very young and lovely makes it so much easier for him to spoil you, if you insist on the word.' Her dark eyes had a musing look for a second or two as she sipped her coffee, then she set down her cup and looked at Corinne directly again. 'You can have no idea, Corinne, what a—a relief it was when Gregori told us that he was bringing home a bride.'

'A relief?'

Irine nodded, her dark eyes earnest. 'To know that he was to marry at last instead of merely——' One expressive hand said so much that Corinne hastily looked away. 'We were all so very pleased about it.'

Corinne toyed with the handle of her cup, and her mouth curved into a rather wry smile. 'Not so much when you discovered that I was a foreigner, though, were you, Irine? Especially not Madame Kolianos!'

Irine, discreet and reluctant to hurt as always, sought for the right words before she replied. 'It is natural for a mother to hope that her child will marry someone—familiar,' she said. 'I hope that my own child will do so, but you are young, Corinne, and if Gregori had married a woman of his own age there would have been—less time.'

Irine hesitated, out of delicacy, to put her meaning any more explicitly, but Corinne knew well enough what she meant and she was less hesitant. Her chin tilted slightly and there was a flush in her cheeks, but she smiled even so. 'Oh, I can imagine that the fact I'm young enough to have a large family must be in my favour as far as Madame Kolianos is concerned,' she said, and laughed shortly. 'But I had hoped to be considered as something more than just the producer of the next generation of Kolianoses!'

'Oh, but of course you *are*!' Irine assured her hastily. 'Mitera takes such matters into account, but not so Gregori; or not so much. He is marrying you because he loves you, Corinne. He loves you so much that——' She laughed in sudden embarrassment. 'Oh, but of course you have no need of my reassurances on that point!'

Corinne's heart beat a little faster as she broached a subject that had often made her curious in the past, but which she had never yet asked about. 'I imagine Gregori's been something of a—a ladies' man,' she ventured. 'He's a very attractive man and at thirty-five he must have had —affairs.'

'You do not mind?' Irine asked, and Corinne laughed.

'I told you, I expect it—I can hardly be surprised with a man like Gregori!'

'You are very wise,' Irine told her with obvious relief. 'Of course you will know what a very virile man he is, much better than I, but I do not believe he has ever *loved* anyone before, although he has been in love. That makes sense, yes?'

Corinne nodded. Although she was much younger than Gregori, her own experience was much the same. She had had boy-friends ever since her early teens, and several times had imagined herself in love. But as Irine said, she had never really loved until that wildly exciting affair with Gregori in Paris. She had been so sure then that it was the real thing and she wished she need not be plagued with such doubts every so often now. If only she *knew* him better!

'Hasn't he ever come close to being married before?' she asked, still seeking to widen her knowledge of him, but Irine did not look at her directly.

'Never to my knowledge,' she said, and put down her empty cup. 'If you have finished your coffee, Corinne, shall we make our way back to the car and go home?'

'By all means.' She looked at the packages they had with them and thought of all the others to be delivered, and shook her head. 'I think we'd better!' she said.

It might simply have been her imagination, but Corinne felt almost sure that Irine had cut their conversation short rather than have her probe further into Gregori's past loves. And as they walked out into the street together she wondered what there was that Irine was reluctant to talk about.

It was rather like burying her head in the sand, Corinne realised, but it always gave her a vague sense of panic whenever wedding plans were discussed, and at the moment it was almost inevitable. So far, apart from going with Irine to buy her wedding gown and trousseau, Corinne had had very little to do with the arrangements for the big day, which was a situation that suited her future mother-in-law very well, for she had a genius for organisation.

Corinne had no family to speak of, so she felt she had very little interest in who attended the traditional feast that would follow the ceremony. She could have invited the Morgans, she supposed, but that presented problems. They were not wealthy people and they all three held down jobs, so that not only would they need to apply for time off but they would also have to spend a great deal of money on fares to attend an occasion that would last for only a few hours. Such considerations might not occur to people like the Kolianoses, but to Corinne with her memories of being a lowly paid secretary, it was a very real concern.

Gregori, on the other hand, had numerous relatives who would all expect invitations, as well as any number of family friends and acquaintances. A wedding was very much a community affair in Greece, and especially in a country area like this. She was so preoccupied with the thought of being the only alien face at her own wedding that for a moment she failed to realise that Madame Kolianos was speaking to her.

'I'm sorry, *madame*.' She brought herself hastily back to reality and smiled an apology. 'I was miles away.'

Evidently the colloquialism was known to her, for Madame Kolianos did not question it. 'That means you are absent in the mind?' she guessed, and Corinne nodded. 'You were dreaming of your wedding, of course.' She did not wait for confirmation, but went on, 'I asked if there was anyone whom you wished to invite to the *dexiosiz*. You have not mentioned anyone as yet, and it is important that the lists be completed very soon. Have you anyone in mind, Corinne?'

It followed so closely on her own thoughts that Corinne did not hesitate about shaking her head; she had already decided. 'No, I haven't, *madame*.'

Madame Kolianos arched her black brows in surprise. 'Your parents are both dead, I believe?' she said, and then seemed to realise how painfully blunt she had been and inclined her head in a gesture of apology. 'Forgive me for speaking so forthrightly,' she said with unexpected humility. 'I did not intend you any hurt, *pethi*, but it is unfortunate when a young woman does not have the support of her family at such a time. Have you no other relatives?'

'Not really.' Corinne wondered just how much Madame Kolianos actually knew about her. Gregori knew little enough, but perhaps he had told his mother even less about her prospective daughter-in-law. 'My mother had a couple of brothers, but I've never met either of them.' She pulled a face, recognising that in the eyes of Madame Kolianos her own case and her mother's were probably comparable. 'Mama was cut off by her family when she married Daddy. He wasn't considered good enough for her and they just didn't bother.'

Her guess had been right, she knew it from the understanding gleam in the older woman's eyes as she displayed definite but tactful interest in the matter while she got on with her meal. 'He was an unsuitable choice?' she guessed.

'They thought so, Mama didn't,' Corinne told her. 'And she was proved right. Daddy was an orphanage child, he never knew who his parents were and he had no money at all when they married; he *never* had any in fact, he was much too unworldly. But somehow they managed to give me a fairly good education and they were sublimely happy together for nearly twenty years. I loved them.'

Her simple declaration obviously touched Madame Kolianos, for there was a look of gentle understanding in her eyes for a moment, a warmth that Corinne had never seen there before. But she was above all else a practical woman, and she was thinking in terms of her only son's future as well as the future of her family's fortunes.

'Happiness is a great consideration,' she allowed, 'but there are more practical considerations to bear in mind when making a marriage, you must realise that, *pethi*.'

Looking at her Corinne wondered how willing a bride she had been. Whether making the best of an arrangement had given her that severely practical outlook, or if she had been born with it. It was the first time she had come close to trying to understand her future mother-in-law, and it surprised her to realise that she was beginning to like her, despite their widely different temperaments.

'I suppose there are other factors to take into account, *madame*,' she agreed with a half-smile, 'but Mama was impulsive.'

'As you are, eh, Corinne?' The bright dark eyes held hers steadily, but it was Gregori who took up the challenge, his deep, quiet voice edged with that chill of steel.

'From whom then do I inherit my impulsiveness, Mama?' he asked. 'Not from you, evidently. And yet it was I who broached the matter of marriage when it had not even entered Corinne's head.'

He had intended it as a defence of her, Corinne knew, and she felt a glow of satisfaction that he came so swiftly and willingly to her aid. Madame Kolianos, however, was not to be defeated. 'I am certain that you are wrong, my son,' she told him with staggering confidence. 'A young girl who has an affair in Paris with an attractive older man almost certainly has marriage in mind. Am I not correct, Corinne?'

How could Corinne answer her? She was not even sure she knew herself what she had expected; she had been sure she loved him, that she would never love anyone else as long as she lived and his proposal had seemed a natural conclusion to a wonderful experience. 'I don't know,' she confessed. 'It all happened so quickly, I hadn't time to think about the whys and wherefores of it, it just happened.'

'And now the wedding is almost upon us,' Madame Kolianos said with a touch of impatience, 'and the guest lists are still not complete. Tell me, Corinne, *do* you have anyone you would wish to invite?'

'No one, thank you,' said Corinne. 'I've decided against asking the Morgans to come over, it isn't really worth their while making such a long trip.'

· She was aware that Gregori had looked up swiftly at the mention of the name, and she knew he was thinking of Robert. His existence had always made him frown, as if he did not altogether like the idea of there being someone like Robert who was so close to her, although he had never actually said anything about it.

Madame Kolianos had noticed her son's sudden interest too, and she eyed Corinne curiously. 'The Morgans?' she asked.

'They're old friends of my parents,' Corinne explained, 'and they were very good to me when Mama and Daddy died. I don't know what I'd have done without them then. Ann and Clifford knew my folks before they were married, and Robert——' She had been going to say that Robert was like a brother to her, but that was no longer true. 'Robert is their son, he's a couple of years older than me, he had his twenty-fifth birthday last month.'

She was talking too quickly and she knew it, but she was much too aware of Gregori's eyes watching her, almost as if he knew of Robert's feelings for her, so recently declared. Madame Kolianos suspected something of the kind too, she thought, and her nodding head suggested she had had some point confirmed.

'Ah!' she said. 'And you have decided against inviting these people to your wedding in three weeks' time?'

Corinne imagined Ann, Clifford and Robert among the alien company that would grace a Kolianos wedding and reaffirmed her decision. 'I think so,' she said. 'I shall visit them later in England.'

Madame Kolianos raised her fine black brows. 'That

will of course depend upon your husband granting permission,' she said, and for the moment Corinne was too preoccupied to resent the suggestion.

'Did you say in three weeks?' she asked. 'I'd no idea it was so soon.'

Madame Kolianos was frowning at her curiously. 'You surely knew of the date?' she said. 'It was arranged before you came here.'

'Yes, I suppose I did.' Corinne laughed and despaired of the shaky sound of it. 'It's just that everything is so —different, I can't keep track of it. I suppose if I'd been married at home, as is usual, I'd have taken a bigger part in the organising and——'

'My son's marriage has very little to do with custom,' Madame Kolianos observed tartly. 'It is taking place with such indecent haste that it is bound to be noticed, and his family did not see and approve the bride before the betrothal! Nothing is as usual in your marriage, Corinne!'

Once more Gregori interposed quickly, taking up the challenge on her behalf, and his eyes glittered darkly with resentment. 'The choice was mine,' he declared firmly, 'both of the bride and the date of our wedding!'

Madame Kolianos was watching her closely, Corinne knew. 'And what of your bride?' she asked her son quietly. 'Does she have a choice, my son?'

Now it was his eyes that watched her, forcing her to look at him, dark and gleaming and showing a hint of the passion that so quickly possessed him. 'It is also my bride's choice,' he assured his mother, and in the circumstances Corinne could not bring herself to deny it.

It was later, when the meal was over, that Gregori came to find her. She sat out in the garden in the warm evening air, surrounded by the heady mixture of scents that were never more exotic than at this time of the day, and she viewed his arrival with mixed feelings.

She could not deny that the sight of him in the brilliance of moonlight brought an urgent flutter to her heartbeat as he came towards her, but he was too disturbing a companion when she had need to think about how little time there was until she married him. In a light suit his dark colouring looked so much more effective, and he had abandoned the tie he had worn for the office, leaving a dark vee of bronzed throat at the neck of his shirt.

He looked at ease, and yet there was something about him that made Corinne certain there was something on his mind. He held a cigarette between his fingers that spiralled smoke as he walked, but he made no attempt to put it to his lips, and as he approached her he flung it from him into the bushes.

'Hmm?' He extended a hand to her and she took it quite automatically, for he had extended that very same, slightly quizzical invitation many times before.

'You do not dislike the idea of walking with me?' he asked, and made Corinne wonder if she had been a little too obvious about her desire to be alone.

'No, of course I don't mind, Gregori.'

She enjoyed the gardens by moonlight, and they were much more extensive than she had realised the first time she saw them. They were so lushly prolific too that it was possible to lose direction unless one was very sure of the geography of the paths. Orange and eucalyptus trees and tall slender cypress formed a barrier between them and the country beyond, and gave her a curious sense of security.

Gregori definitely had something on his mind, she had no doubt of it now, and she glanced at the strong profile that looked so much more primitive in the moonlight. His hand enclosed hers and his strong gentle fingers squeezed lightly every so often as if to convey a message. He raised it to his lips when he caught her looking at him, then pressed it to his breast over the throbbing urgency of his heartbeat.

'You do not wish your friends to come to our wedding?' he asked, and, taken by surprise, Corinne did not answer at once.

'I—I thought it might be better not to ask them,' she said.

'You have some special reason for not wanting them here?'

She tried to tell herself that he could not possibly know about Robert's feeling for her, but it was a curious thing to have asked, and she frowned up at him. 'You might find it hard to understand,' she said in a slightly husky voice, 'but they can't afford to fly all this way just for a few days, and I doubt if they could all get the necessary time off from their jobs either, in the time.'

'And you think I would not understand that?'

'I don't know.' She glanced up at him briefly. 'I didn't know what you meant by a special reason for not asking them.' She shook her head. 'That's it, you see, I don't really *know* you as well as I should know the man I'm going to marry in three weeks' time.'

They were in the fragrant shadow of an orange tree when Gregori brought them to a standstill with his hands on her shoulders. 'I know *you* well enough, my lark,' he said, and his voice had the caressing softness of velvet.

'Do you?'

He bent and kissed her lips; a light lingering kiss that promised all the passion and excitement she knew him to be capable of. 'I believe so,' he said. 'Although there are times when you puzzle me, I confess.' He was smiling; a glimpse of white in the darkness of his face, and his hands either side of her head threaded their long fingers through her hair, running gently and caressingly through its silky length. 'Three weeks is not too soon for you, is it, my lark?' he asked softly. 'Are you not as impatient as I am for us to marry?'

So many times Corinne had asked herself the same question, and never yet had she known the answer. Nor did she now, as she kept her gaze on the firm curve of his mouth rather than meet his eyes. 'I don't know,' she confessed, and the hands that had been so caressingly gentle held her firm for a moment and tipped back her head so that he could look into her face with bright gleaming eyes that looked as black as jet in the moonlight.

'Then I must convince you, my love, must I not?' he said, and brushed her mouth with his lips. 'I wish only to please you. If you would like your friends to come to our wedding, then I will see that they are flown out here as our honoured guests. Is that what you would like?'

His generosity was staggering, but Corinne could not see Robert as anything but a very unhappy spectre at the feast in the circumstances, and to invite Ann and Clifford without him would be to invite comment. Nevertheless she found it curiously affecting to realise what lengths he was ready to go to to please her.

Impulsively she reached up to kiss him. 'That's very generous of you,' she told him. 'It wouldn't be possible for several reasons, but thank you for thinking of it.'

'I wanted to please you, my lark, that was all,' he whispered. 'I love you.'

He curved a large hand around her cheek, and his eyes

when they looked at her as they did now reminded her of other moonlight nights, so that she shivered with pleasure at the memory. He put his arms around her, drawing her close until she tipped back her head and looked up at him.

His lips brushed her neck, muffling the soft words of his own tongue in the thickness of her hair. Then he sought her mouth and kindled the same wild rapture she had yielded to so often in the past. Lifting her arms, she encircled his neck and drew the dark head down even closer, her body responding to the urgent desires of his. She could not think beyond this moment and nor did she wish to.

With only four days until the wedding, Corinne felt disturbingly restless as she looked out at the pine trees hemming in the house on all sides. The past two and a half weeks had passed alarmingly quickly, but with Irine as her almost constant companion it had been difficult not to get caught up in the excitement of the preparations.

The wedding gown had been delivered; and it was a far more extravagant one even than she had realised, but it was being brought home to her at every turn that nothing but the best was good enough for a Kolianos bride. The honeymoon must needs be brief, so Gregori had informed her with obvious regret, because unfortunately he had an important business meeting to attend only five days after they were married.

Sometimes Corinne wondered still whether she was doing the right thing, and yet she had done nothing to try and call it off and go back home. One reason, she told herself, was because she simply did not have enough money for the fare home, and she refused to be indebted to the Kolianos family for that. Restlessly she turned back into the room and on the spur of the moment made up her mind to go out alone. So far she had never gone anywhere alone; she had always had either Gregori or Irine with her, although it had never been suggested that they were there to ensure her return.

It was fresh outside despite the warmth of the sun, and it did something to soothe her mood as she strolled on down through the gardens and into the surrounding pines. They smelled delicious and the air was delightfully cool under the trees with only the occasional sound of a bird to disturb the quiet, and the faint shush of the ocean on the far side of the road.

There were no fences and the trees ran almost to the edge of the road, giving free access to anyone who had the wish to walk through them, and Corinne was nearing the road when she noticed a car parked only a short distance off to her left. It was because there was something vaguely familiar about it that it held her interest, and she was looking at it with a curious prickling sensation running across her scalp when someone called her.

'Corinne!'

She turned sharply, her eyes wide, when she recognised the voice, realising at once why the car had looked so familiar. Robert came through the trees almost running in his haste, and took her hands, looking into her face for a moment before he said anything. The familiarity of him caught at her breath for a moment and she felt a slight mistiness in her eyes.

'You're all right?' he asked anxiously, and she nodded hastily.

'Yes, of course I'm all right, Robert!' She laughed a little breathlessly. 'I'm just so staggered to see you here, that's all. Are you all here? Clifford and Ann too?'

'No, I came alone. I took every scrap of leave I could get!' He held her hands tightly and for a moment did nothing more. But there was something in his eyes that she took heed of and she tried to free her hands and move away slightly. He kept hold of her, gripping her fingers more tightly, then raising them to his lips he kissed their tips. 'I had to see you, Corinne!'

She was still too startled to know exactly what to say or do, but she had a very good idea of what was in his mind, and another declaration of love from Robert was something she felt she could not cope with at the moment. 'Where are you staying?' she asked, desperately trying to avert the inevitable. 'There aren't any hotels very near here.'

'Oh, I'm fixed up; not on the mainland. I haven't sorted myself out yet, but I've got the car with me and —well, to be quite honest I drove in this direction first to see if I could find the place. I've come straight from the airport. Mad, I know, but I *had* to try and see you!'

'It was rather impulsive of you,' Corinne told him, but felt a certain gentleness because he so obviously had her welfare in mind.

'The car ferry that's to take me across to the island wasn't due for a couple of hours, so I had plenty of time.' He made the explanation as if he already regretted his impulsiveness. 'I don't know what the island roads are like, or how often I'll be able to get over again, or even if there are any roads, but——' He stopped short and stood looking at her for a moment or two with his earnest grey eyes. 'Oh hell, Corinne love, you know why I'm here! You must be in absolutely no doubt.'

Corinne managed to free her hands and she walked off just a short step, enough to put distance between them before she turned and looked at him. 'I have a very good idea,' she agreed, and desperately sought the right words for what she had to say next. 'And although it's lovely to see you again, Robert——'

'You wish I hadn't come!'

'I'm being married in four days' time,' she told him, and Robert stared at her, then took her hands again, gripping them even more tightly.

'Four days?' he echoed. 'Oh no, Corinne, you can't, not that soon! Oh, my poor silly darling!'

'It isn't as terrible as you seem to think,' she told him. She had her own doubts, heaven knew, any amount of them, but she was not prepared to have Robert add his to them, and she shook her head at him. 'And anyway, it is more or less a *fait accompli* now. The wedding gown, all the arrangements—everything. Only an earthquake can stop it now.'

'Then damn it, *I'll* stop it!' Robert declared fiercely. He drew her to him so that she was conscious of the tense urgency of his body when he put his arms around her and held her close. 'I love you, Corinne, and I'm damned if I'll stand by and see you throw yourself away on a stranger! I realise how hard it is for you to get away, I should never have let you come here, but I can get you out of it and I will! You're coming back to England with me!'

Feeling rather as if she had been plunged out of the frying pan and into the fire, Corinne had no time to state her own feelings before Robert gathered her even closer in his arms and sought her mouth with a hungry eagerness. Her struggles stemmed more from instinct than desperation and she broke away, breathing heavily, when she recognised the voice that cut suddenly across Robert's whispered endearments.

'You are Robert Morgan, I suspect,' Gregori said clearly and distinctly, and the quietness of his voice carried the cutting edge of steel. A veritable furnace of anger burned behind the dark eyes that regarded them so steadily. 'Won't you introduce me, Corinne?'

How he was managing to control a so obviously violent temper amazed Corinne and she moistened her own dry lips anxiously before she did as he said. 'Robert is the son of Ann and Clifford Morgan who I told you about, Gregori,' she said. 'Robert, this is Gregori Kolianos.'

'Soon to be Corinne's husband,' Gregori informed him with an unmistakable threat in his voice. 'Are you perhaps in Greece for our wedding, Mr Morgan?'

Their handshake was merely a concession to formality. Robert was angry and also outfaced, for he had allowed himself to behave as he would never have done in normal circumstances. He disliked being found in the situation that Gregori had found him in, Corinne suspected, almost as much as he disliked the idea of her marrying, no matter how defiant he looked.

'If I have my way there won't *be* any wedding!' he declared, and Corinne pressed a hand to his arm before he could say more.

'Please, Robert,' she begged, 'don't say any more! Don't make a scene, please!'

He said nothing, responding to her plea or perhaps deterred by the look in Gregori's eyes. For a second or two he watched her face, as if he tried unsuccessfully to determine what her feelings were, then he turned abruptly, muttering something that she did not catch, and walked back to his car with a curiously stiff-legged gait that expressed his anger better than words could have done.

Corinne watched him go with undeniable regret as well as relief, for she liked Robert, she was even fond of him. If only she could have loved him it would probably have made everything so much more simple. As the sound of his car receded into the distance, she turned and found Gregori right behind her, making any hope of escape unlikely.

A firm hand on her arm added to the thudding beat of her heart and she looked up into his face with a strange feeling of mingled fear and excitement. 'Why did you not tell me that there was another man, Corinne?' he asked, and his voice betrayed just how angry he was, no matter how well he had managed to control it so far. Then his fingers tightened suddenly and his eyes blazed in the rugged darkness of his face. 'Oh, *kólasizi*, Corinne! Are you never to be honest with me?'

'There *is* no other man!' She made the denial swiftly and without hesitation and believed it had the desired effect. Shaking free of him, she walked off, rubbing at the marks his fingers had left on her arm. As she turned to face him her eyes seemed dark, shadowed by the pines that kept out the sun. 'I've known Robert ever since I was a little girl, all my life practically! I had no idea that he felt the way he does until I was on the point of leaving to come here; he drove me to the airport. He tried to stop me coming; he said he loved me, that he'd always loved me, but until then I didn't know! I *didn't* know!'

It was difficult to avoid his eyes when he watched her so steadily and she turned away after a moment and stood with her back half to him. 'You went out with him? In those weeks while I was away?'

His voice followed her, deep and insistent, and she looked at him with a spark of defiance in her eyes. 'Yes,

of course I went out with him, I saw no reason not to!
Robert is good company and when it was so long—I
thought you'd forgotten all about our—affair!'

'An affair?' Gregori managed somehow to convey reproach without changing the pitch of his voice and she
stirred uneasily. 'Is that how you think of it, Corinne?
Is that how easily you can dismiss that very special thing
we had in Paris?'

It was dangerous ground and she recognised it, turning her shoulder to him defensively. 'I haven't forgotten,
it's just that it's—it's different. I had time to think in
those five weeks when I didn't see you and I began to
realise that the whole situation had been vaguely un-
real.' There was a kind of appeal in the glance she gave
him while she rubbed a hand absently over the shoulder she kept so firmly turned against him. 'You know
as well as I do what a reputation Paris has for romance,
and especially in the springtime. It went to my head—I
believe it went to both our heads, Gregori.'

'But not to our hearts?' She glanced at him quickly
and caught the deep dark gleam in his eyes. 'You really
believe that, Corinne?'

He was beside her and she felt herself trembling when
he put his hands on her shoulders and turned her towards him. There was the same burning desire in his
eyes and the same wild excitement in his nearness that
there always was. His hands had the same gentle, per-
suasive touch, his lean body the thrilling touch of fire
that she knew so well and she shook her head only half-
heartedly when he lifted her face to him and sought her
mouth.

What seemed like an eternity ago in Paris, he had put
his brand on her, seared it into her senses until she knew
she would never be free of it, no matter how often she

doubted or how often she shied away from the day that
was much too close for comfort now. His mouth touched
her lips lightly, coaxing them apart, then crushing them
with a bruising fierceness that aroused every nerve in
her body.

His passion kindled her own, as it had always done,
and she looked at him with eyes that were glowingly
soft and shining when he raised his head for a moment
to look at her. 'Is it so very different from Paris, my lark?'
he whispered.

Her thoughts only lightly touching on Madame
Kolianos's dark watchful eyes and Zoe's defiant antagonism, Corinne shook her head, then lifted her mouth once
more to his kiss. She knew in her heart that she was
too easily persuaded, that tomorrow she would still have
the doubts that plagued her, but at the moment nothing
seemed to matter very much except being in Gregori's
arms, and she yielded as she always did.

CHAPTER FOUR

It was when Corinne was driving back from Athens the
following day with Irine that she spotted someone just as
they turned into the approach road to the house; just a
glimpse of someone half hidden among the close-standing
trees. She glanced hastily at her companion to see if she
had noticed anything, but apparently Irine was oblivious,
although the chauffeur turned his head briefly, as if he

too might have noticed it.

Almost inevitably Corinne thought of Robert, and all the time she and Irine were unpacking their purchases she kept thinking of his unexpected appearance yesterday in the same spot. Suppose he had come to try and see her again; could she find it in her heart to pretend he wasn't there? It was a question that plagued her all the time they chattered happily about the things they had bought, and showed them off to the other three women in the family.

It was another half-hour before she eventually succumbed to temptation and took another stroll down through the gardens as she had the day before, and on towards the road, through the pine wood. It was possible she had been mistaken, but she did not think so; it was Robert waiting down there, she felt almost sure, and she simply could not find it in her heart to ignore him.

She had walked almost as far as the road and seen no sign of him when she caught sight of a sudden movement further back in the trees and swung round quickly. It was almost a relief when Robert stepped out from the shadows and came towards her, walking slowly as if he was a little less sure of his welcome today. And she guessed the quick darting glance he gave behind her was to check that Gregori was not following on her heels.

'I've been here for ages,' he told her before she had time to say anything, and eyed her with obvious anxiety. 'I came over early and caught a bus—I can't get the car in the boat I've borrowed.' He half-smiled and she found it so touchingly familiar that she was glad she had followed her instincts and not simply left him waiting there. 'Am I forgiven, Corinne?'

Smiling, she allowed him to take her hands but skilfully evaded the kiss he would have pressed on her lips, receiving it instead on her cheek. 'There's nothing to forgive,' she told him, 'but I'll forgive you if it makes you feel better, Robert.'

'You knew I was here?' He eyed her curiously. 'I saw a car go up to the house more than an hour ago and I thought it looked like you in the back with another woman.'

Corinne nodded. 'That was Irine, Gregori's sister-in-law; we'd been shopping. I saw you as we turned in.'

'And you slipped out to see me again?'

He obviously read some significance into it, and Corinne shook her head. 'I could hardly leave you standing around out here all day,' she told him. 'Although you're not being very wise roaming about among the trees, Robert, you could be mistaken for a prowler. Yorgo, the chauffeur, saw you as well, I think, and if he says anything——'

'They'll set the dogs on me!'

'Nothing as dramatic as that,' Corinne denied. 'But it is necessary to be a bit security-minded in a place like this, Robert.'

She found him difficult to understand in this mood, he made her uneasy. He gave a brief and unmistakably baleful look in the direction of the house and shrugged. Quite obviously he had something to say and having given him the encouragement of coming out to see him, Corinne supposed she had little option but to hear what it was. At her suggestion they walked along under the trees, just a little way in from the edge where they could not be seen from the road, although she had not consciously sought to hide away.

Reaching for her hand suddenly, Robert squeezed her fingers tightly. 'I'm here for a long time, Corinne; I've taken every day due to me, in one go! It wasn't easy, but

I managed it, and I've rented a house on Damos, one of the smaller islands. The natives are very friendly there, and I've borrowed a boat from one of them.'

'Oh, but that's lovely for you, Robert!' Corinne was doubtful about the effect of his presence on her own situation, but she did not want to appear as if she took it for granted he was there for her sake alone. 'You'll love the islands, they're beautiful!'

'So I believe.' The hand that held hers tightened its grip, and a glance at his face showed him frowning deeply. Then he brought them to a standstill and turned to face her so that she could see how darkly serious his eyes were. 'I haven't just come to enjoy myself, my sweet, you must realise that. I've come to try and persuade you to come home with me. No, no, no, don't turn me down out of hand, listen to my plan first! I'm willing to give up the holiday if you'll just let me help you out of this—this trap you're in. I can, I have an idea and I know it will work, but I need your co-operation.'

'Robert, please—I'm not in any trap.'

'It's a trap!' Robert insisted stubbornly. 'Mink-lined and very luxurious, no doubt, but you're trapped, my sweet, and I know how to spring it. By getting at Kolianos through his precious pride! With what I have in mind he'll be only too glad to let you go!' He smiled and raised a brow. 'You don't actually dislike me, do you, love?'

He knew very well that she did not dislike him, but nor did she want to become involved with him in the way he so obviously intimated. It was staggering to discover that Robert was capable of planning some kind of scheme to force Gregori to let her go, and she felt a moment of dismay that he had become so unfamiliar suddenly.

'I don't know what you have in mind,' she told him, 'but I'm not interested in any scheme to free me, as you call it. I'm not looking for a way out that's likely to cause Gregori or his family any kind of embarrassment—I'm not sure I'm looking for a way out at all. I may not be absolutely sure that I love him as I thought at first, but —well, I definitely don't want to hurt or embarrass him either.'

Robert's face was flushed and earnest and there was a smouldering look of resentment in his eyes that made them appear shifty; a fact that was another disturbing change for the worse. She placed a hand on his arm and shook her head, seeking to placate him without yielding to his suggestion concerning Gregori.

'I know how you feel, Robert,' she told him. 'You know I'm still unsure at times, and you dislike Gregori——'

'I hate his guts!'

His vehemence startled her so much that she blinked. 'Well, you shouldn't,' she insisted. 'After all, I did agree to marry him quite willingly in the first place, and you can't blame him for making sure I don't jilt him!'

Clearly he did not understand her, but after a moment or two he apparently resigned himself to the fact that she was not going to change her mind, and he shrugged. 'O.K., I won't mention it again! I accept that you're prepared to go like a lamb to the slaughter and there's nothing I can do about it! We're still friends?'

Corinne smiled her relief. 'Yes, of course!'

He took her arm and together they strolled back through the trees. 'Good! But if you won't let me rescue you, will you at least find time to spend an hour or two with an old friend before you become the lady of the manor?'

'Oh, I shan't be lady of the manor,' she denied. 'Madame Kolianos is firmly established in that role.'

Catching a tone in her voice, Robert raised an enquiring brow. 'A dragon?' he suggested, but Corinne hesitated before confirming it.

'She's a very strong and a very brave woman,' she said after a moment or two. 'She received some kind of an honour from the Greek government for her wartime work. But I have the feeling somehow that despite that stern exterior I'd be very happy to have Madame K. behind me in a crisis.'

Robert squeezed her hand and brought her back to matters more important to him. 'Will you come and see my island hideaway, Corinne? Just for a couple of hours; I'll get you back in time for dinner.'

It was a temptation to go somewhere other than the shops in Athens with Irine and Iole, and it could not possibly do any harm. She chose to ignore the fact that Gregori would certainly oppose the trip if he knew of it, and told herself that she was still mistress of her own life for a few more days yet.

'I don't see why not,' she said. 'I'll have to pop back to the house for a handbag and to let them know I'll be out for the rest of the day; after that I'm free.' She could see the question in Robert's eyes and answered it quickly and with a touch of defiance that he noted with a brief smile. 'Gregori's at the office in Piraeus, and he won't be home until this evening.'

Robert kissed the tips of her fingers before he let go of them. 'Good,' he said. 'Then I'll wait here for you, there'll be a bus along very soon.'

The island was smaller than Corinne expected, but enchantingly picturesque, and she thought it delightful the

way the one and only village straggled upwards from a
tiny quay. Fishermen's cottages clustered closest to the
quay, and one or two farm cottages up on the higher
ground where the land was more arable.

'It's like a Lilliput island,' Corinne told Robert when
he took her up to the highest point of the island to show
her the view. 'And you're the only visitor.'

He seemed well pleased with the situation. They had
lunched on bread and cheese and a bottle of rough but
palatable local wine, up on the hilltop, and now they
made their way back down to his rented house. Small,
with only three rooms, it was primitive but spotless,
despite the lingering smell of fish.

'Unless you decide to stay I'm the only outsider,' he
told her as they entered the tiny cottage, and Corinne
shook her head firmly. Sitting himself on the edge of the
table he sighed resignedly. 'You really mean to go
through with the marriage?'

Corinne traced a line with her finger-tip along the edge
of the table. 'All the arrangements have been made. The
feast is being prepared and the priest primed in English
as well as Greek so that I know exactly what's going on;
there's no going back now, Robert. In three days' time
I shall become Kiría Kolianos.' She laughed a little
wildly when she thought of being Gregori's wife, for it
gave rise to a thrill of excitement as well as those never-
ending doubts.

Robert, still perched on the edge of the table, reached
for her hand and held it tightly. 'And then I'll have lost
you,' he said, and his voice was not quite steady.

'We'll still be——'

'I'll have *lost* you!' he insisted, and Corinne shifted her
gaze uneasily.

It dawned on her then how much she risked by being

there with him at all, and the afternoon had sped by so quickly. Picking up her handbag, she eased her other hand free and glanced at the watch on her wrist. 'I really think it's time we thought about getting me back to the mainland, Robert,' she told him. 'I've enjoyed seeing your island and it was lovely to sit on the hilltop and have lunch, but it's getting rather late, and——'

'Yes, I suppose it is.' It was quite clear how much he disliked the idea of taking her back to Gregori, but he shrugged and eased himself from the edge of the table. 'O.K.,' he said. 'You're the boss! It wouldn't do for your Greek to come home from his honest toil and find you missing—especially in the circumstances!'

His bitterness made her anxious, but she did not see what she could do about it at the moment. 'I would rather be there before Gregori gets home,' she said quietly. 'then I can tell him myself.'

Robert's eyes were evasive as he took her hand while they walked down to the quay. But having helped her aboard the borrowed boat he set about fiddling with switches and buttons, taking so long about it that Corinne frowned at him curiously, and eventually got up to go and see what he was doing.

'Is something wrong?' she asked, and her heart was beating with sudden urgency.

Wiping his hands on a rag, Robert shrugged. 'I'm afraid we're out of fuel, love. I'm sorry.'

Corinne stared at him for a moment, unwilling to believe it, but he was already out of the boat and reaching down a hand to help her on to the quay beside him. 'Robert, it can't be as final as that,' she protested. 'Surely someone can let you have some fuel, can't they? There must be a—a depot or something.'

'There's no depot,' Robert assured her, 'and these

people use their boats to make their livelihood, Corinne. Every drop of fuel is brought in from Piraeus and there's a delivery due tomorrow. I can't ask one of them to give up his precious fuel supply so that I can take my girl-friend home. I'm sorry, love, but you're stuck until morning, there's just nothing I can do about it.'

'But there must be *something*!'

She was filled with an unreasoning panic suddenly as she looked around at the other small boats in the harbour. Already most of them were preparing to set out for the night's fishing and she had to concede that Robert had his priorities right. But she was too stunned by the unexpectedness of it at the moment to think of an alternative; all she could think of was Gregori's re-action when he found her still missing when he arrived home. It was almost as if Robert might have planned it to happen that way.

She gave him a swift sideways glance suddenly as he guided her across the quay and back towards his cottage, speaking impulsively. 'Robert, you didn't do this on purpose, did you?'

'Don't you trust me?' There was an edge of bitterness on his voice and his smile lacked warmth, so that she feared she had hurt him with her suspicion. 'Oh, I admit I might have done it if I'd thought of it,' he confessed with a short laugh. 'All's fair in love and war, you know, my sweet, and it's really not much different from the classic situation of the car running out of petrol and the girl having to walk home to save her honour, is it?'

Corinne was looking across at the mainland, growing less clear in the already fading daylight, and she frowned anxiously. 'Except that I can't walk home,' she said.

It was almost dark and the sunset had left splashes of

red and purple in its wake, staining the rocky headland of the island that Corinne could see from the tiny kitchen window. They had to eat, as Robert pointed out, and preparing a meal at least gave her something to do and stopped her dwelling on what was happening in the Kolianos home right now.

Gregori would be home by now and she shivered involuntarily when she visualised his reaction. He would have been told where she had gone and who she had gone with, and she knew in her heart that he would be hurt as well as angry, although she would not have admitted it was that that she regretted most.

The sudden pounding that shook the planks of the cottage door startled her so much that she dropped the knife she was using and stared over her shoulder as Robert first frowned curiously, then got up to go and answer it. But he had scarcely time to open the door before Gregori came into the room, brushing past him as if he did not exist.

He came straight through into the kitchen to where Corinne still stared in stunned amazement, with the kitchen knife on the floor at her feet and her hands clasped loosely in front of her. His face was dark with fury and his eyes glittered blackly like chips of jet when he looked at her.

'Gregori——'

Her explanation was cut short when he seized her wrist in a bruising grip that brought a cry of protest from her, and an angry flush flooded into Robert's face. Gregori turned and walked back towards the door, dragging Corinne with him and pulling her round in front of him with a sharp tug, as he turned to glower at Robert.

'Who the hell do you think you are to come barging

in here?' Robert demanded. 'Dragging Corinne off as if she was——'

'I came for the woman I am to make my wife in three days from now,' Gregori informed him harshly. 'I know that does not meet with your approval, Mr Morgan, but it is a fact and there is nothing you can do about it!'

'Gregori, will you please listen to me!' Unexpectedly he turned and gave her his attention, and Corinne moistened her lips anxiously before she began. 'I came on a trip to the island with Robert——'

'Even though you knew I would not wish you to?' he demanded, and brought a flush of resentment to her cheeks.

She angled her chin defiantly, daring him to dictate her actions. 'I do still have a freedom of choice,' she reminded him, 'and Robert is an old friend. There was no harm in coming over to see his holiday cottage and having a picnic on the hilltop—I enjoyed it. I made no secret of where I was going or who I was going with, and when I told Zoe I'd be back before evening I meant to be! Only the boat Robert borrowed ran out of fuel and there was no more available; not until morning when the supply boat comes over.'

'So you intended to stay here all night with him?'

She avoided the glittering darkness of his eyes uneasily. 'I hadn't much option,' she said.

Gregori said something in Greek, and looked at her with a searing look of scorn in his eyes. 'Are you too foolish to see that he had planned this deliberately?' he demanded. 'Or were you a willing partner in this—charade?'

Corinne stared at him. It had occurred to her briefly in the beginning that Robert had contrived the situation to suit his own ends, but she still found it hard to believe

that he would resort to such tactics, let alone have the
nerve to carry them off. But Gregori was impatient, and
he once more took her along with him to the doorway.

'Now wait just a minute! Not so fast!'

Gregori swung around to face him and Robert took
a half-step back before the fury in his eyes. His face had
such a savage fierceness that it would take a brave man
to stand against him, and Robert's present stand arose
more from stubbornness than bravery.

'Do you deny that you planned this—this venture
with the intention of bringing disgrace to my fiancée?'
Gregori demanded, and Robert retreated a step further.

Nevertheless he found the nerve from somewhere and
his grey eyes had a dark glittering look that was quite
alien to the man that Corinne knew. For the first time
in all the years of their friendship, she felt he was a
stranger to her.

'For your information,' he said, 'Corinne came with
me quite willingly—and I mean *quite* willingly!'

He pressed on relentlessly. Having offered her a way
out, it seemed he meant her to take it, willing or not. In
his way he was as single-minded as Gregori when he was
bent on getting what he wanted, and she found the
revelation too much to cope with at the moment.

'It surely tells you *something*,' Robert insisted, driving
home the point. 'Damn it, Kolianos, a man like you
doesn't want to marry a woman who's made it as plain
as she can that her interests lie elsewhere!'

'Oh, Robert, no, please don't go on!'

Her own faint protest apparently went unnoticed, but
for a moment Corinne thought Gregori was going to hit
him, she had never seen him so coldly furious, and the
strong fingers that encircled her wrist tightened their
grip briefly until they almost stopped her pulse. Then

he glanced down at her and his hold eased a little, though he still retained his grip on her.

'Since you appear to have such a clear insight into my character, Mr Morgan,' he said to Robert in a quiet voice that belied the stormy darkness of his eyes, 'you must surely understand that—a man like me?—must claim back his own or risk losing face. I cannot allow another man to kidnap my bride and get away with it, you must see that.'

Robert's gaze shifted uneasily, although in the brief moment he glanced at her Corinne saw anger still lurking there. 'What are you going to do?' he asked, as if he expected some form of retribution, and Gregori narrowed his eyes for a moment as he stood there in the doorway with Corinne held fast by one hand.

'To Corinne?' he enquired softly. 'It is the custom for —a man like me to beat a runaway wife.' His eyes scorned the idea of any possible chance of it happening in this case, and Robert turned hastily away, his face brightly flushed. 'The same rule does not apply to fiancées, however, so you have no cause for concern, Mr Morgan! Another few days and the outcome might have been different!'

As he finished speaking he turned on his heel and, taking Corinne with him, went out into the night; striding off down to the quay as if he was just as impatient to get away from the situation as Corinne herself was. The quay itself was almost deserted, but there were sounds of voices and laughter coming from the *taverna* on the waterfront, and figures hurrying past them in the half-dark spoke a greeting that Gregori responded to automatically. It was such a normal, peaceful scene that Corinne found it hard to believe the violent eruption of temper back there had really happened.

She knew that Gregori owned a motor launch that he kept in the harbour at Piraeus, but this was the first time she had seen it and she noticed how gleamingly white and sleek it appeared on the dark waters of the little harbour. It surprised her rather to discover a crewman at the wheel, but it was Gregori who helped her aboard. He gave the man an order, then bent to unloose the mooring rope, but paused suddenly and straightened up, so that the man at the wheel looked at him curiously.

'*Éna lepto!*' Gregori told him, and the man shrugged when he went striding off along the quay.

Most of the boats that used the harbour were out, but the rather ancient motor launch that had been loaned to Robert was moored only a short distance from them, and Corinne's heart thudded in anxious dismay when she realised Gregori's intention. His air of purpose was unmistakable, and he jumped down into the boat without hesitation, then stood for a moment before the wheel, presumably taking stock of the strange craft.

The crewman leaned against the wheel watching him, curious but unconcerned. But not so Corinne; she waited with bated breath for that traitorous engine to spring to life, and sure enough she started suddenly when it began to chug hoarsely in the evening still. It ran for no more than a second or two, but she listened to it with tears in her eyes because she realised that an old friend had deceived her all along, for his own ends.

Having proved his point, Gregori came back, striding along the quay looking as lean and dangerous as a big cat. Bending to loose the mooring line he coiled it in one hand while he leapt aboard, then nodded curtly to the crewman. '*Az pãme!*'

Corinne hastily brushed away her tears as the engine of their own launch hummed richly, sweeping them astern across the island harbour, then turning in a wide arc before picking up speed. Corinne, standing in the stern, watched the lights of the *taverna* wink across the darkness, a brisk wind snatching at her hair and blowing it forward about her face.

She realised Gregori was close by when the smoke from his cigarette drifted across her face, and she stiffened herself for the onslaught she felt sure must come. He had not even stopped to put on different clothes, but still wore the business suit he went to the office in; merely dispensing with the formality of a tie as he normally did the moment he got home. Obviously he had stopped only to learn that she had gone to the island with Robert, and then come immediately to fetch her back.

Even without physical contact she could feel how taut and angry he was still, and her heart thudded hard. An emotion between fear and excitement overcame the sense of despair that Robert's deception had aroused in her. It would be almost a relief when the storm broke, and she waited with her hands clenched tightly on the rail.

'I despise liars, and most of all I despise bad liars!' His voice took on a curiously unnatural flatness out there on the ocean, and she started nervously when he sent the end of his cigarette spinning over the side into the water.

Corinne did not look at him, instead she kept her eyes on the receding lights of Damos and the shimmering ruffles of white that followed in their wake. Nor did she answer him, not even to object, and after a moment or two he went on, almost as if he found a kind of relief in berating her.

'Did it not occur to you how easily I could check that unlikely story simply by starting the engine?' he asked, but still she remained silent, driving him to further accusations. 'You intended to stay on that island with him!

You intended to spend the night with that man!'

'Robert! His name's Robert!' Desperation drove her to find her voice at last. 'I stayed only because I thought I had no choice. Robert told me we couldn't get off until morning and I believed him because he's a friend—an old friend.'

She sounded so desperate because she had need to convince herself of it after the last few minutes. But Gregori was too burned up with his own anger to notice that her protest also had a note of anguish. 'Have you not heard of the telephone?' he demanded, and she stared at him blankly for a few seconds, then shook her head.

'I didn't—*is* there a telephone on an island that size?'

Gregori made a short impatient sound with his tongue. 'Do you also believe that we are still in the Middle Ages? Like that man who is your lover? Was it in the hope of making me so angry that I would free you from your promise that you did this, Corinne? Did you hope to shame me into giving you up?'

'Oh no, there was nothing like that at all, I swear it!' Her voice quivered and tears stood in her eyes once more, because she was almost sure that Robert had meant to do just that, and she hated to have to admit it, even to herself. 'I trusted Robert! Can't you imagine how *I* feel? He promised to get me back by the time you came home and I had no reason to doubt him! When he said the fuel had run out and there was no more available, how could I argue with him? I didn't know he was lying to me!'

Even without looking at him Corinne could imagine the look in those deep dark eyes as they watched her. 'And did you imagine that hearing no word from you and knowing you were over there with Robert Morgan, I would do nothing about it until morning?'

She should have known he would come for her,
Corinne realised, because he was worried about not
hearing, if for no other reason. 'I should have known
you'd come,' she acknowledged.

'Of course you should! How would I know whether
or not you were safe? There were a thousand and one
reasons why I would come for you, Corinne, not least
because I feared you——' He shook his head quickly.
A long gentle finger lifted a tear from her lashes, then
she heard him sigh and the cooling of his temper was
like the passing of a storm. 'I believe your incredible
innocence because I want so much to believe it,' he said.
'It is my weakness that I cannot stop trusting you!'

'But you *can* trust me!' Looking up at him she saw
that in the greenish glow of the starboard light, his skin
took on a curiously metallic gleam. He looked like a
bronze sculpture, with a godlike ruthlessness that was
alarmingly affecting. 'You needn't doubt that I'll marry
you as I promised in three days' time,' she told him. 'I
shan't break my promise!'

He gripped his fingers tightly about her upper arms
and his eyes glittered in that uncanny green light. 'Indeed you will not, my lovely!' he vowed. 'No matter
what your friend may have suggested I would do if he
kept you there with him, I have no intention of letting
you go! You love *me*! How can I doubt it when each
time I hold you in my arms you burn with a passion as
fierce as my own? Do you think I could lose you now?'

'I've promised,' she said again, in a voice so small it
was barely audible above the hum of the engine as the
boat sped across the water to Piraeus.

'And will you also promise never to cause me such
anguish again as you did by going off with Robert
Morgan today?'

'Anguish?' She looked up at him questioningly, for it seemed so strong a word to use, but Gregori pulled her close into his arms and looked down at her, his eyes glowing darkly in that face of sculpted bronze.

'How could I be sure that you had *not* gone away with him?' he demanded harshly. 'Do you think it was only my pride that was hurt, Corinne?'

His arms crushed her with steely strength as fierce as the ardour that burned in his eyes, and Corinne shook her head slowly back and forth. Twining a hand in the silky thickness of her hair, he held back her head and exposed the vulnerable softness of her throat, murmuring words in his own tongue that conjured up warm spring nights in Paris. Then he bent his head and plunged his mouth into the soft hollow of her throat, his lips searingly fierce on her cool skin.

With a little sigh of surrender Corinne reached up her arms to him, and her body responded as it always did to the wild desire that only he could kindle. He took her mouth with an almost brutal force and her spirit soared exultantly into a world of sublime ecstasy. He had pride in plenty, but how could she doubt that he loved her too? She would marry him in three days' time, but not only because there was no other way for her.

CHAPTER FIVE

CORINNE could recall the past few hours only in a kind of daze. The church that was much too small to accommodate all the relatives and friends as well as the inevitable people who simply loved a wedding, and especially when they could anticipate a good feast afterwards. The Kolianoses were wealthy and the tables would be well-laden and the wine flowing freely.

A cousin of Gregori's had acted as his *koumbáros*, holding garlands of leaves above their heads while they stood at the altar. The exchanging of rings, the chanting of the priest and then the traditional three circuits of the lectern while the guests threw flower petals, streamers and rice; it all seemed so much like an exciting and noisy dream that Corinne found it hard to believe it had actually happened.

The sound of the bells still seemed to ring in her ears, high and thin above the musicians' jigging accompaniment that led the dancing people all the way back from the church. It seemed to Corinne that the whole village had attended their wedding, as well as the uncles, aunts and cousins she had been introduced to but since forgotten because they were so numerous.

She had expected excitement, but not the kind of excitement that these garrulous, lively people injected into the occasion, and she had drifted through it all like someone in a dream. Everyone had agreed, although Gregori had needed to translate the compliments for her, that she was a beautiful bride in the white silk and lace gown that she and Irine had chosen.

A veil and a coronet of flowers covered her thick auburn hair. The traditional offerings of money were pinned to both the veil and her gown, covering her with the symbols of wealth from head to foot and fluttering distractingly each time the light wind caught them. The wine she had drunk in answer to repeated toasts had given her a strange feeling of unreality, and she found it hard to realise that the occasion that she had shied away from so determinedly only weeks ago was at last a reality. She was actually Gregori's wife.

The sounds of excited Greek voices, and of laughter thickened by generous draughts of wine, followed her as she went into the house and upstairs to her room. The room that would no longer be hers when she returned from a brief honeymoon, but which she was to use for the last time to change out of her bridal dress.

Irine was to have helped her change, into a soft pale green dress that Gregori had chosen especially for her, because it flattered her red hair and green eyes, he said, but at the last moment Corinne had asked to be allowed to do it alone. Irine had complied although obviously the request puzzled her.

Outside in the gardens every available space seemed to be taken up with tables laden with food and drink, and it was noisy. The happy sounds, traditional on such occasions, but which made Corinne feel disturbingly alien when so much of the talk going on around her was in a language she could not understand.

Already, as she mounted the stairs, the peace and quiet of the big house had a soothing effect, and she made her way along the carpeted landing without hurrying. There was time enough before she and Gregori left for their four-day honeymoon, but she had given herself plenty of time, as she was changing without Irine's help.

Her footsteps deadened by the carpet made her aware suddenly of the sound of someone moving on the landing ahead of her and she looked up, vaguely surprised, at the young man who moved swiftly away from her. She had no idea where he had come from and she did not recognise him; but then most of the people at her wedding were strangers to her, and she looked at him, only vaguely curious.

It was almost as if they sensed one another's presence in the same moment, for he turned his head suddenly and looked over his shoulder at her. She had a fleeting impression of panic in his dark eyes before he hurried on, almost running now and making for the back stair. A narrow flight that gave access to the garden via the servants' living quarters.

'Just a moment!'

Calling after him was purely instinctive and prompted by his air of stealth, but he did not attempt to stop, only said something in Greek which she could not have understood anyway, even had it been audible. Instead he went more quickly than ever and began the descent in quick anxious steps, until he disappeared from her sight.

Not concerned enough to bother herself further, Corinne went on past the bedroom doors, until one of them opened suddenly as she passed and Iole came out. It must have been her imagination, but it seemed in that first instance that Iole looked slightly taken aback when she saw her, and her eyes shifted uneasily.

Corinne was never quite sure how to deal with Gregori's niece, for it was difficult to get close to her because of that more or less permanent air of resentment and defiance. Whatever it was had caused the near-quarrel between Iole and Gregori on Corinne's first day there had presumably been forgotten by everyone except Iole, for Corinne had never heard it mentioned again.

'You've soon changed out of your finery,' she said, with a hopefully friendly smile.

Following tradition, Iole had been one of the unmarried girls attending the bride, wearing coronets of flowers and carrying beribboned candles. The rest of the girls still wore their finery while they mingled with the guests downstairs, but apparently Iole had dispensed with hers as soon as possible. She looked only slightly discomfited by the question and shrugged carelessly.

'I hate dressing-up,' she said, and caught Corinne's eye with that unmistakable glint of challenge and defiance. 'You don't mind, do you, Corinne?'

Taking a leaf out her book, Corinne too shrugged and shook her head. 'No, of course I don't mind,' she said. 'Why should I?' A recollection of the figure she had seen on the landing came to her then and she attempted another subject. 'You didn't see anything of a mysterious young man wandering around up here earlier on, did you?' she asked. 'I saw him on the landing along there and he bolted like a rabbit for the back stairs when I spoke to him.'

Iole's eyes were wary again and hastily avoided hers. Shrugging once more with the carelessness that only one of her race could convey, she made to move past her. 'Oh, heaven knows,' she said. 'It was just one of the guests, I expect. The house is teeming with people for this wedding!'

'I just wondered who he was,' said Corinne, but Iole was already making for the main staircase and did not even turn her head.

Watching her almost run down the stairs, Corinne shrugged as she turned to go to her own room. As Iole said, the house was teeming with people and she herself knew very few of them; it was quite possible, she supposed, that Iole did not know them all, and yet—— She shook her head as she opened her bedroom door. She did not understand Iole, nor did she think she ever would, but she had other things to think about at the moment.

There was a comforting familiarity about her room that was rather surprising when she considered she had occupied it for barely more than seven weeks. Maybe the fact that she would no longer have the privacy of a room of her own after today made her view it differently.

Almost without exception, whenever she came into this room she went straight across to the window and looked down into the gardens at the back of the house. But today the scene differed enormously from its customary peace and quiet. From above the wedding feast appeared to have been embroidered like a tapestry against an exotic background of shrubs and flower borders, and the whole bright picture framed in dark pines that clustered protectively around it.

Nearest to the house, the pool, like an opulent blue gem in its setting of white marble, was an oasis of quiet and cool. Beyond that the laden tables, and the guests in their best clothes; the small orchestra of bouzoukis and guitar plucking out traditional songs and dances wove a bright pattern of colour in the fierce sun.

The garden door from the kitchen was directly below her and as she started to draw back a movement caught her eye. It must be an absolute hive of activity in the kitchen today and they must be falling over one another as they scurried back and forth replenishing the feast. Possibly it was an attempt to remain unseen while he made his way through the kitchen that had delayed the departure of the young man she had seen on the landing earlier. For Corinne had no doubt at all that it was him she saw creeping stealthily away, and she leaned forward to see more clearly.

His clothes precluded the idea of his being a temporary hired help, and if he was one of the guests, as Iole suggested, then he could be expected to make his way back to the wedding feast, but he did not. Instead he made directly for the corner of the house nearest to him with such unmistakable stealth before disappearing from her sight into a thick border of shrubs that she began to wonder if she ought to tell Gregori about him, in view of the number of wealthy guests at the wedding.

What caused her to hesitate was an impression she had gained that, despite her denials and apparent casualness, Iole knew who he was. Corinne stood before the mirror and removed the coronet of flowers from her head, complete with the veil and a shower of fluttering paper money, then ran her hands over the lace dress, similarly endowed, while she gazed absently at her reflection.

She began to unpin the notes as she recalled her first introduction to Gregori's family. Iole had protested indignantly at being referred to as a child and declared that no matter how long she was married to Costas Menelus, the man designated as her future husband, she would never forget—— And at that point Madame Kolianos had silenced her.

But was Iole quite as subdued by family insistence as she appeared to be, or did she have some of the same stubbornness that her uncle showed when it came to choosing a life partner? Corinne wondered. Perhaps now that she was Gregori's wife she should take a more responsible view of Iole's rebellion, but she could not find it in her heart to condemn her for her attitude.

Looking at her own reflection for a moment in the long mirror she ran her hands once more over the exquisite white lace, then shook her head suddenly and pulled it downward, and off over her hips. From now on she had quite enough to anticipate in the matter of her own future as Gregori's wife, without becoming involved in Iole's problems. And if the young man had been to see her, it was Iole's concern.

The pale green dress was perfection, and she spent a moment admiring her husband's undoubted good taste. The colour was complimentary without making too bold a contrast with her auburn hair, and it fitted her firm young figure with the seductive flattery of pure silk. Such expensive luxuries were, she supposed, something she would come to accept as a member of the Kolianos family, but she doubted if she would ever become blasée about it.

Her dressing completed, she came downstairs once more and was half-way across the hall to rejoin the wedding feast when Iole came in from the garden. Through the open doorway behind her the big oval pool glittered in the sunlight, forming a barrier of quiet between the house and the sounds of revelry in the gardens beyond, so that Iole had no need to raise her voice to make herself heard. From the way she looked as Corinne approached her, it was clear that she had something to say, and she stopped when they drew level.

'Corinne——'

Iole's dark eyes often reminded her of Gregori's. They were huge and sultry and set between similar long thick black lashes, but it was not usual to see them look as appealing as they did now. She looked far more than her seventeen years, in a rather sophisticated dark red silk that gave her a gypsy look, and also emphasised the fact that she would not always be as gauntly slim as she was now.

But it was that look of appeal that Corinne noticed, and for the first time since their initial meeting she felt the kind of sympathy for her that an older sister might. 'Iole, is something wrong?'

The girl glanced over her shoulder, but no one seemed yet to have realised that the bride had reappeared, and the laughter and the talk went on. 'I have something to ask of you,' Iole began, and it was obvious that she found it hard to confide in her. 'When you saw that man upstairs——' She broke off abruptly, biting her lip.

'*Signomi*, Kiría Kolianos.' Corinne turned swiftly, momentarily startled to hear herself addressed by her new title, and the manservant who had used it smiled faintly at her response. '*Signomi, kiría*, but there is a caller for you in the salon.'

'A caller?'

Iole was momentarily forgotten as she frowned at him curiously. He had an inexplicable air of reticence, she thought, and it puzzled her for the moment. He glanced at Iole, but when Corinne turned to apologise to her the girl was already leaving them, making her way back to the party.

Disappointed to lose what had promised to be a confidence from her newly acquired niece, she was nevertheless too intrigued by the man's message to call after her, and Corinne shrugged resignedly. 'Who is it, Vassos?' she asked, and the man lowered his voice quite obviously when he told her.

'It is an English gentleman, *kiría*, who says he is a friend.'

Corinne's heart gave a breathtaking leap suddenly and she looked at the man uncertainly, grateful nevertheless for his discretion. 'A Mr Morgan?' she asked, and Vassos nodded agreement.

From his eyes it was obvious that the arrival of this strange man claiming to be a friend of the bride, but not an invited guest, puzzled him. But he had taken care that he gave her the message as discreetly as he could, and Corinne gave him a brief smile of thanks. 'Thank you, Vassos, I'd better see him. But——' she hesitated, wondering just how far the man could be trusted, 'I'd rather no one knew that I have a visitor for the moment.'

He nodded his understanding, obviously intrigued by the behaviour of his employer's new bride. 'I will tell no one, *kiría*,' he vowed, then glanced across at Iole's tall straight figure as she skirted the pool on her way back to the party. 'But I do not know if Thespinís Iole——'

'Oh, you needn't worry about that,' Corinne assured him swiftly.

Unless she was very much mistaken, Iole was in no position to carry tales. Following the man's information, she went into the house again and made for the main salon where she expected to find Robert waiting for her, and she told herself as she went that she was not deceiving Gregori. She was simply making sure that he was not upset by her very natural desire to say goodbye to an old friend.

When she first opened the salon door it struck her how alien Robert looked in this big and rather severely luxurious room. He was wearing a suit and not a tee-shirt and slacks as he had been when she saw him last, and she approached him with a certain reticence. He noted the pale green dress and his eyes showed appreciation of Gregori's taste, but he did not attempt to kiss her or even take her hands. Instead he simply stood and waited for her to cross the room to him, outwardly calm, until she noticed the wariness in his eyes.

'Hello, Corinne.' He did not smile either, and she felt rather sad suddenly at seeing him so formal and obviously ill at ease. 'I suppose I should address you as Madame Kolianos now.'

'Kiría Kolianos.' She corrected him automatically, then shook her head. 'But of course you don't stand on ceremony, Robert. I'm still Corinne to you, surely, I haven't changed that much in three days.'

Standing with his hands thrust into the pockets of his jacket, he said nothing for a moment, then shrugged uneasily. 'The last time we saw each other I tried to—make things difficult for you. I'm sorry, Corinne. I was jealous, I'm still jealous, but I hope I'm a little more sane than I was then. I came to say—I came to wish you every happiness. I hope you'll be very happy, even though I still think you've done a foolhardy thing, marrying that man.'

'We'll see,' she said softly. 'But thank you for your good wishes, Robert; I know they're sincere.' She felt discomfitingly close to tears suddenly and she must not cry or it would give him quite the wrong impression. 'Won't you come and join the——' Her voice trailed off when she realised what she was suggesting. 'No. No, of course not— I'm sorry, I didn't think.'

'It wouldn't be a very good idea,' he said.

'You're going home?'

He hesitated a moment, then shook his head. 'Not yet,' he said. 'I've got plenty of leave, so I might as well make the most of it. I doubt if I shall ever have another opportunity to spend so long in the Greek islands.' He fixed his eyes on her face for a moment and she noticed how darkly grey they looked. 'You'll be going away yourself?'

he guessed, and there was a tight, clipped sound to his voice.

'Only for four days; Gregori has to attend a business conference, so we have to come back.'

Robert drew breath to say something else, but like Corinne he had caught the sound of someone coming through the hall, and the firm tread of a man in a hurry was enough to tell them both who to expect. Robert gave her a swift look that apologised for once again making things difficult for her, and Corinne shrugged. Maybe it was coincidence, or perhaps Iole was less afraid for her own secrets than Corinne thought.

When the door opened and Gregori stood framed in the opening for a second or two, it was clear that the sight of her visitor took him by surprise. His black brows drew swiftly into an instinctive frown above that glitteringly fierce look that Corinne was by now so familiar with. But as always he showed remarkable self-control.

'I was unaware that my wife was entertaining a visitor,' he said with deceptive quietness, 'I came merely to see why it was she had not yet returned to me. Good morning, Mr Morgan; will you not join the rest of our guests in the garden?'

Robert's mouth tightened ominously, and Corinne prayed that he was not going to say something that they would both regret. 'No, thanks,' he said shortly. 'I just came to see Corinne.'

'Ah!' The gleam in Gregori's eyes was unmistakably satisfaction. 'You are leaving Greece?'

'No, I'm not,' Robert declared firmly. 'I'll be around for quite a while yet. I just wanted to have a word with Corinne, that's all.'

'But not, I imagine, with the idea of congratulating her

on her marriage,' Gregori guessed, soft-voiced, and Robert's mouth hardened into a straight, tight line.

'You're damned right!' he confirmed harshly. 'The last time I saw her you were dragging her away like a stray dog, and I don't trust you any further than I can throw you, Kolianos! I wished her happiness, but I haven't much hopes that she will be, with you!'

'Oh, Robert, no, please don't—not today of all days!'

Corinne made her plea in a small and not very hopeful voice, for she had never known Robert be so quick to anger, or so determinedly quarrelsome as when he and Gregori came into contact. And when she saw the dark fury in her husband's eyes she wished fervently that she had been sensible enough not to see Robert alone.

'I'm sorry, Corinne.' Robert's jaw looked square and stubborn and she had little hope that he was going to change his opinion to please her. 'You know my opinion of this—this marriage, and I still think you've been coerced in some way.'

'No, I haven't!'

'I assume you have said your goodbyes,' Gregori's voice cut across her anxious protest. 'You will now leave, Mr Morgan.' His eyes glittered blackly, and he raised his voice just slightly to forestall the objection that Robert was about to make. 'And in future you will have the goodness to stay away from my wife; do I make myself clear?'

'Like hell!' Robert breathed angrily. 'Your wife, as you call her, is an Englishwoman and you can't keep her under lock and key! You can't lay down the law about who she sees and doesn't see!'

'On the contrary,' Gregori told him in a voice like chilled steel, 'my wife is now Greek, and Greek women obey their husbands! I repeat, Mr Morgan, you will not see my wife again, nor will you attempt to communicate with her until I say so. You will leave my house and I shall give strict orders that you are not to be permitted to enter it again!'

'Gregori!'

Corinne's own small protest went unheeded, but Robert was standing his ground. Perhaps he regretted the fact that matters had got so out of hand, but he was not yet prepared to yield; Gregori, she knew, would never yield on the point that he was within his rights to bar whom he liked from his home. 'So that's it?' snapped Robert. 'Well, trying to isolate Corinne from her friends won't work, Kolianos! Not with me, it won't!'

It could go on indefinitely, Corinne thought, desperate to bring it to an end, and she spoke up once more, determinedly. 'Please stop it!' she begged. 'This isn't doing any good—it's pointless!'

Robert stared at her as if he saw a different side to the situation suddenly, and he was shaking his head as he thrust both hands into his pockets. He would find it hard to understand her apparent lack of appreciation for his concern. 'I'm sorry,' he said after a moment or two. 'I suppose I'd better go before I make things any worse for you, Corinne.' His eyes switched again briefly to Gregori, his meaning unmistakable. 'But I'll be around for a few weeks yet, and if you need me——'

Corinne shook her head, not trusting herself to speak, while Gregori watched with his mouth set firmly and his lean body as taut as a bow-string. 'You will not be troubled, Mr Morgan,' he said. 'I am well able to take good care of my wife.'

Obviously Robert was of a mind to argue the point, and probably would have done if he had not caught Corinne's pleading look. Instead he shrugged and turned abruptly to go, sending a parting shot over his shoulder as he made his way across the room without even saying goodbye to her. 'You'd better!' he said.

The salon seemed incredibly quiet after he had closed the door behind him, and almost immediately Gregori reached for a cigarette; a means of relieving the tension of the last few minutes. Corinne watched, fascinated, while a steady hand applied the flame to its tip and the strong passionate face was briefly illuminated.

Its hard primitive lines, a deep cleft in the chin and a strong brow and jaw, were softened by shadowy black lashes, and it never failed to amaze her just how many different emotions this man could arouse in her. Anger and excitement were too often akin to make it easy for her to put her feelings for him into any kind of a niche, but he could be comfortingly reassuring too, and certainly there was little chance of their relationship ever becoming dull or stale.

'If you are ready to leave,' said Gregori his quiet voice breaking into her résumé, 'our friends are waiting to wish us luck and to see us on our way.'

His friends, Corinne mused a little ruefully, for he had just remorselessly sent packing the one face familiar to her. 'Yes, of course,' she said, snatching her thoughts swiftly back from self-pity. In the circumstances, and taking Robert's determinedly aggressive bad manners into account, she could not blame him for reacting as he had, although her own understanding surprised her for a moment. 'I brought my handbag downstairs with me,' she told him. 'It's in the hall with my luggage, if Vassos has fetched it yet.'

His smile had a hint of irony that was vaguely discomfiting. 'You do not realise how events have moved along while you were with——' He used one big hand to dismiss Robert's brief presence. 'Our baggage is already in the car. I am anxious to be away, Corinne, that is why I came to look for you.'

And found her with Robert instead of in her room, Corinne thought ruefully. 'I had to see—I mean I couldn't *not* see Robert——' she began, and caught her breath in the second before he smothered her words with his mouth.

With his big hands either side of her face he looked down at her. He was smiling, but there was a firmness about his mouth that told her he meant exactly what he said. 'I do not wish to hear that name ever again, Corinne, hmm?' He kissed her once more, tempting her with the promise of passion in his mouth, then he took her arm, smiling with the look of a man well satisfied. 'Now we will say goodbye to our friends and begin life together, eh, *ligho éna mou*?'

It was a prospect that brought a thudding urgency to her pulse suddenly as he led her across the hall, for with a brief flutter of panic she realised for the first time that there was no going back now. She had made her choice and Gregori would see to it that she never left him again; he had made a vow to that effect and she knew him well enough to be certain it was no idle threat.

The light was dazzling outside after the coolness of the salon, and the clamour of voices poured over them the moment they were seen crossing the hall. Faces flushed with good wine and smiling broadly, surrounded them as they left the house, and but for Gregori's arm Corinne might have shrunk back. Bright garrulous voices called out good wishes in a meaningless jumble of sound until he translated for her, whispering the traditional sentiments close to her ear.

'They wish us long life and many sons,' he murmured,

and when she glanced up his eyes were gleaming with an expression that brought colour to her cheeks and a breathtaking wildness to the beat of her heart. 'We hope that they are right, eh, *ágapitikós mou*?'

He pulled her round into his arms suddenly and in front of them all kissed her more tenderly than he ever had before, but for so long that when he eventually raised his head she clung to him breathlessly. With the approving cheers of the well-wishers ringing in her ears she was lifted off her feet suddenly and carried out to the car, Gregori's arms tightly possessive about her, his dark and smiling face benign with satisfaction.

Placing her with loving care into the front seat of the car, he went striding round to take his place beside her. For a moment he gave his attention to starting the car and making sure it was running smoothly, then he turned and looked at her enquiringly. Corinne half-smiled, her gaze held boldly by those gleaming dark eyes, then he turned in his seat and pulled her to him once more, and this time his kiss was harder and more forceful, leaving her breathless. With a deep, soft laugh he let her go and turned to start the car, while Corinne coped with a moment of wild shattering excitement. As they drove along the curving, pine-shaded road she never gave another thought to Robert.

Not until their flight was called had Corinne had the slightest idea what their destination was to be, and when Gregori took her arm and moved towards the departure gate when the Paris flight was called she had looked up at him in swift and unmistakable pleasure.

His expression showed that he had hoped to please her with his surprise, and Corinne's reaction could have left him in no doubt that he had succeeded. Obeying an impulse, she had thrown her arms around his neck and kissed him, bringing a smile of understanding to the faces of a couple who almost collided with them when they stopped so suddenly.

She recalled the incident now and smiled over it yet again. This brief honeymoon would perhaps give them the opportunity to get to know one another better. Paris had the same magic still, and she smiled to herself as she looked out of the hotel window at the lights and the shimmering dazzle of water in the distance. It gave her a warm, comforting glow to see it all again, and she wondered how she could ever have considered Gregori anything but the perfect lover, when he conjured up such delightful surprises for her.

They had said little on the flight over; it was as if they were oddly shy of one another since they became man and wife, and yet there was a rapport that made their silence a comfortable one. It was only now, as she stood in the hotel window thinking about the most eventful day of her life, that she remembered Robert again and the implications he had made about the sort of husband Gregori would be. Not that she believed them, of course, but as she stood there looking out at the Paris night, she realised just how little she did know about the man she had married.

She half-turned from the window and Gregori was coming out of the bathroom, his lean length wrapped in a towelling robe whose shortness left his long muscular brown legs bare. He had washed his hair while he showered and was towelling it dry as he walked into the bedroom, so that it was tousled and curly, making him appear oddly vulnerable for a moment.

Catching her look he smiled, a slow and infinitely sensual smile that sent thrills of excitement running through her. 'You look beautiful,' he said, and his voice was several tones lower than it normally was, and shiveringly seductive. 'But why do you look so solemn, my lark? What do you have running around in that busy head of yours, eh?'

Finding her own responses too overwhelming for a moment, Corinne turned back to the window and pushed one of the curtains aside so that she could once more see the lights of Paris. Very careful to keep her voice steady, she ventured to tell him at least something of what had been on her mind.

'I was just trying to decide how much truth there was in things I've heard,' she told him. 'Like—will I really be expected to obey you now that I'm married to you? Are Greek wives really obedient to their husbands?'

Gregori was silent for a moment, but she could sense him watching her, as if he was trying to judge just how serious she was. 'Does the idea displease you very much?' he countered, and she took a moment to admit it.

'It wouldn't work with me,' she told him frankly, 'nor with any modern-thinking woman, I imagine. But *is* that how Greek men still treat their wives? Or were you and Robert just saying that?'

'Robert?' She heard the change in his voice and her heart fluttered warningly. 'Have I not said that I do not wish to hear his name mentioned again, ever?'

'That's exactly what I mean,' Corinne insisted, and turned round to face him again. 'Am I to have no say in what I do or who I speak to from now on? Do you intend to bully me until I'm too frightened to say or do anything without first asking my husband's permission?'

Gregori got up from the end of the bed, where he had been sitting while he towelled his hair dry, and he came across to her, running his hands through thick curls that gave him a much more primitive look than usual. 'Are you frightened of me, Corinne?' he asked, and his voice had the caress of a velvet glove so that she half-closed her eyes in response to its seduction.

'I will be if you go on laying down the law as you did today,' she told him, and noticed how small and whispery her own voice was.

'I do not believe it!' He put his hands on her shoulders, his long fingers stroking her soft skin under the silk nightgown she was wearing. 'You will never be afraid of me, for you have spirit; and I have no wish to break your spirit.'

She turned her head slowly from side to side as he caressed her, and put her hands to his chest, feeling the warmth of his flesh through the towelling robe, fresh-smelling and damp from the shower. He bent his head and found her mouth, forcing back her head as he kissed her and sliding his arms round to draw her close.

His mouth still on hers, he reached down and lifted her into his arms and carried her across to the bed, then laid her down on it gently. She reached up and put her arms around his neck as he lay down beside her, looking up into his face for a moment, her eyes slumbrous and heavy-lidded and her mouth seductively smiling.

'But you will expect me to be obedient and cut myself off from my friends if you say so?'

Her head was spinning with the wild uncontrollable beat of her heart, and she was not really interested in anything but the lean muscular body that was pressed so close to her side. Her voice was a husky whisper that trembled each time he kissed her cheeks or her half-closed eyes with their long thick lashes. Then he sought her mouth again, and the soft spot beside her left ear, his face buried in the richness of auburn hair that muffled his words.

'Can you think of another man at a moment like this?'

he demanded, and she laughed breathlessly as she pressed her lips to the strong brown column of neck, pushing back the loosened robe he still wore from the bronzed nakedness of his body.

Only an irresistible desire to hasten the inevitable made her answer as she did, for she knew how he would react. 'I didn't say Robert particularly,' she said.

Gregori raised his head and his dark eyes had a depth-less glowing blackness that filled her with wild longings she did not even try to control. 'That man!' he muttered in a deep rough voice, and shifted his weight. 'You will forget him, *ágapiménos*—I will make sure of it!'

'Gregori——'

She was half laughing and half fearful when he took possession of her mouth and her body with the fierce exultant strength of a conqueror, and suddenly every-thing and everyone was forgotten in the passionate, in-toxicating joy of becoming his wife.

The four days in Paris had recaptured everything of their first rapturous weeks together and added something much more exciting, and when they took off on the flight home to Greece Corinne gazed down at the hazy shimmering city below them with an irrepressible sense of regret. Nothing would ever be quite so wonderful again, and she wanted to prolong it as long as possible.

Gregori had spoken to her twice and had to repeat himself, and he squeezed her hand with his strong fingers, frowning at her curiously when she gave him her atten-tion. 'You are sad, my lark?' he asked softly, and she admitted her mood with a rueful smile.

'I hate leaving Paris,' she told him. 'All the most wonderful things that have ever happened to me have happened there.'

He kissed her finger-tips and smiled, his dark eyes sharing her memories. 'We will come back one day, my love,' he promised. 'It will still be here!'

'But what I mean is,' Corinne tried to explain, 'that it can't ever be quite the same again.'

He held her hand tightly and there was a look in his eyes that told her he regretted the truth as much as she did herself. 'It is the way of things, my lark, that honeymoons have to come to an end and lovers return to earth. But as long as we have one another it is still enough, is it not?'

'I hope so.'

Not only her words but the sound of her voice made him put a hand to her cheek and turn her face towards him while he frowned over her slightly apprehensive expression. 'Oh, Corinne, you are not still doubtful that you have done the right thing by marrying me? How can you doubt it after these past few days, eh?'

'I love you, but there's still an awful lot about you that I feel I don't know.' She looked at him with large serious eyes and hoped he knew what she was trying to say. 'We've known each other a very short time, Gregori, and—— Oh, of course it will be all right!' She delivered herself a swift scolding, while Gregori held her hand and obviously found her lingering doubts cause for concern. 'I'm being idiotic making so much of it! Lots of people marry after even shorter affairs than ours! It's just that —to your family I'm still an outsider and it's that that makes me so reluctant to go back. I can understand their point of view in one way——'

'You are my wife,' Gregori insisted firmly, and kissed her so determinedly that a stewardess hastily changed her mind about offering them drinks and moved on. 'Young as you are, my love,' he whispered as he held her hand tightly and close to his heart, 'you must learn to take your place as my wife and not allow yourself to be—overshadowed. Mama will soon love you. I know it,' he added with a quick smile, 'because she already admires the way you stand up to me! That is the right phrase, is it not?'

Corinne nodded, but found it hard to believe his assessment of his mother's opinion. 'I find that hard to believe,' she said. 'I would have thought she was a staunch supporter of tradition. The dominant role of the male included!'

'Papa was traditional,' Gregori informed her with a gleam of mischief in his dark eyes because he was enjoying her obvious surprise. 'He kept a very tight rein on all his family, but since he died Mama has—what is it?— taken the bit in her teeth. She likes to rule us all with a firm hand, just as Papa did, and I do not always make myself popular by going my own way. She had placed so much faith in my brother Dimitri's ability to take over Kolianos and Company, you see, and she was distraught when he died.'

'But she still has one son. She still has you.'

She reached up to stroke a hand down his cheek and the touch of his smooth dark skin sent little shivers of excitement through her. Taking her hand and turning his mouth to her palm he pressed his lips to it, his head bent while he kissed her lingeringly, his eyes close and holding hers steadily.

'And God willing, she will soon have a grandson also,' he whispered. 'Then Mama will worship you as a goddess, my beautiful love, you will see!'

CHAPTER SIX

USUALLY Corinne was up in the morning before Gregori left for his office in Piraeus, but occasionally it happened that she was a little late, like this morning, and when that happened she hurried over bathing and dressing with one eye on the time. Madame Kolianos had an intense dislike of people staying too long in bed, other than when they were ill, and too long lingering was likely to produce an enquiry if the latecomer to the breakfast table was unwell.

Their return to Greece seemed to Corinne rather an anti-climax, but as Gregori had pointed out to her, even lovers had come down to earth some time. Despite his assurances on the plane coming home, there had been no sign that Madame Kolianos was any more kindly disposed to the idea of her as a daughter-in-law, and she doubted if she ever would be, although Irine was unfailingly pleasant and kind. It was possibly her awareness of being a stranger in a foreign land that lent an added sense of loneliness when Gregori was not there with her.

It was so hot as she bathed and dressed that she began to think longingly of the Pont Neuf in Paris and shady walks beside the river, and small cafés under the leafy spread of plane trees. Whatever else happened during her married life, those four days honeymooning in Paris with Gregori would remain the happiest of her life.

Still sunk in nostalgia, she made her way along the landing, and gasped aloud when a door opened suddenly just as she was passing, snatching her relentlessly back to the present. The room was Iole's and she saw the girl hesitate in the doorway for a moment, unresponsive to her smile. Then she noticed that the normally glowing dark skin was pale and sallow and there was a look in Iole's eyes that drew her sympathy, even though they were hastily averted.

Reaching for her hands, Corinne looked at her anxiously. 'Iole, whatever's the matter? You look ill!'

'I am not ill!'

The swift denial made Corinne frown at her curiously, for very obviously it was not the truth. Whatever her reasons, her paleness and seeming uncertainty concerned Corinne enough for her to take advantage of her few years' seniority for once, and she took Iole by the hand and led her back into her room, sitting her down on the bed.

'You're definitely not well,' she stated firmly. 'Have you got a pain somewhere?'

'No pain,' Iole insisted.

'Then what is it?' Corinne urged, placing a hand on the girl's slightly damp forehead. 'You don't seem to have a temperature.'

Iole's eyes were still evasive and she shook her head. 'I have been a little sick, that is all.'

She made the admission so reluctantly that Corinne frowned at her again, still puzzled by her attitude. Quite clearly Iole would much rather she was not there, and looking as she did it would have made more sense if she had welcomed company, whoever it was.

'I'd better fetch your mother.' Corinne grasped at the obvious solution and stared in surprise when, far from expressing relief, Iole showed signs of panicking.

'No, no, no!' She pulled her hands free and scowled like a disobedient child at her. 'I do not wish Mama to be informed, nor Yayá; especially Yayá! I forbid you to tell anyone, Corinne!' Her huge eyes were raised briefly in appeal and they reminded her so much of Gregori's that Corinne found the appeal irresistible. 'Please, Corinne, I do not wish them to know.'

'All right, but it doesn't seem very sensible to me.' Corinne was horribly unsure whether she should succumb to the plea, but there was a little more colour in Iole's cheeks even though she still looked much too pale, and she was obviously troubled by something, for it showed in her eyes.

'What made you so ill?' she asked, trying to establish a possible minor stomach upset, even though such a cause was unlikely to make Iole so edgy.

'It is nothing.'

The reply was as evasive as the dark eyes that looked anywhere but at her, and Corinne was unconvinced. 'Maybe you should see a doctor to be on the safe side,' she suggested, but that suggestion too was blocked, with such vehemence that it startled her.

'I will not see a doctor!' Once more that trace of panic aroused Corinne's suspicion and she frowned. 'I will *not*, Corinne!'

A persistent suspicion niggled at Corinne's mind as she tried again to hold that evasive gaze and she sat down beside Iole on the edge of the bed, regarding her steadily while she spoke. 'How often has this happened before, Iole?'

Iole made no reply but kept her head downcast after one brief, burning glance of dislike, but her expression said it all. The air of mingled defiance and pathos and the determinedly averted eyes strengthened her suspicion until Corinne could no longer doubt it. Putting a hand to the side of Iole's face, she turned her to face her, but

Iole jerked her head and defeated her.

'How often, Iole?' she asked, as gently as she knew how, but still the girl said nothing, and she sighed inwardly. '*Are* you pregnant?' she insisted, and Iole nodded.

In the circumstances it was strange, Corinne thought, that her first thought, her first sympathy was for Gregori. He had cared for Iole ever since his brother died, and protected her as if she was his own; loved her just as deeply, and she could imagine just how hard this would hit him. He was a proud man as well as a loving one and he valued his family's good name; a good name that Iole, by her folly, had put in jeopardy.

'Your boy-friend?' Corinne pressed for the rest now that she knew this much, and once more Iole admitted it.

'I want his child because I love him!' she declared with childish stubbornness, but her bottom lip was slightly unsteady when she said it, and it brought out all Corinne's protective instincts.

'Will he be prepared to marry you?' she asked, and a sudden flush of colour in Iole's cheeks reminded her of how quickly the other girl was recovering.

'I am not allowed to marry him,' Iole said with a thrust of her bottom lip. 'They have arranged that I marry Costas Menelus!'

Corinne was in fact aware that the arrangement was not as definite as that. Both families hoped for a match when Iole was a little older and everything was being done to move things along in that direction, but so far it was no more definite than that.

Corinne had met Costas a couple of times and liked him. He was quite good-looking and rather shy and he adored Iole unreservedly, but it was perhaps because of his obvious devotion that Iole, with the perverseness of her sex, refused to even countenance him as a future husband. Whoever the father of her baby was he had made certain that the families' marriage plans did not include Costas Menelus, and Corinne wondered if Iole was perhaps feeling a lot less certain of herself at the moment.

'Surely things will be different now,' Corinne suggested. 'Now that you're—the way you are, the situation is quite different.'

'Do you think so?' The bright dark gleam in Iole's eyes made her uneasy, and Corinne thought for a moment before she answered.

'I don't know for certain, of course,' she said cautiously, 'but I would think it made a difference.'

'You would say so to Thíos Gregori?'

The question took Corinne by surprise and she stared at her for a moment, made more uneasy by the obvious glint of appraisal in the dark eyes that watched her. 'I don't know about that,' she admitted after a second or two. 'I really don't want to get involved in anything like this so soon after I've joined your family, Iole. This is something you should discuss with your mother and get her to put your case to Greg—your uncle. You must tell her, Iole.'

'No, not yet,' Iole insisted firmly.

She was on her feet now and pacing up and down with the nervous energy of a young tigress, her bright dark eyes fully alert now and challenging in the brief glance they gave in the direction of Corinne, who still sat on the edge of the bed and watched her uneasily. She was much different from the girl that Corinne had found pale and unsteady in the doorway of her room, and of the two of them she was far more sure of herself.

'Will you promise not to tell my secret to anyone?'

She had stopped in front of Corinne and stood looking down at her, and Corinne hesitated, horribly uncertain. 'Iole, I don't know——'

'For just a little while longer,' Iole insisted.

It was difficult to see what use it would be to delay the moment when it would soon enough become imperative to tell someone. Glancing at that youthfully angular figure she recalled her speculation on the day of her wedding, that Iole would not always be so gauntly slim, but she could have had no idea then just how soon her speculation would be a fact.

'There is time enough yet,' Iole assured her, almost as if she had followed her train of thought. 'In the meantime you will not tell anyone else, eh?'

How difficult it was, Corinne thought despairingly, to resist the demanding appeal of those dark, compelling Kolianos eyes, and she heaved a sigh of resignation as she shook her head. 'I ought not to,' she said, 'but I'll promise to keep your secret as long as I'm able, Iole. But only on condition that you do not wait too long—for your own sake.' Iole nodded and smiled, but Corinne was already wondering, as she got up from the edge of the bed, how long it would be before she regretted making her promise.

Both Zoe and Iole were out somewhere and the big salon was unusually quiet. Madame Kolianos sat reading and she frowned her dislike at the sudden shrill interruption of the telephone. Irine got up to answer it while Madame Kolianos removed her spectacles and sat listening to her monosyllabic answers and frowning. Eventually she got up from her chair, and it was obvious to Corinne that something was wrong.

Seeing Irine's face when she turned, Madame Kolianos

hugged her close before putting her at arms' length to eye her questioningly. 'Tell me, *pethí*,' she said. 'Tell me what has happened.'

Her quietness inspired courage, and after a moment or two Irine did as she was bid, although her voice was still noticeably unsteady. 'There has been an accident,' she said, and only extreme politeness and consideration for Corinne could have made her speak English at a moment like this. 'Iole has been injured and also the young man who was driving the car she was in.'

Madame Kolianos muttered in her own tongue while she piously crossed herself, then she turned and picked up the house telephone. 'I shall come with you to the hospital, naturally,' she said in her firmest voice, and broke off to speak rapidly in Greek, obviously giving orders. 'While we await the arrival of the car,' she went on, turning back to her daughter-in-law, 'you will tell me about this accident, eh? How badly is the child injured?'

The dark eyes gave the clue to her anxiousness, but the firm voice betrayed nothing, and Irine told her as much as she knew herself. 'I know only that she is hurt, Mitéra, not badly, I think, but she must stay in the hospital.'

'Ah!' Satisfaction at her granddaughter's escape was overshadowed by a bright curious glitter in her dark eyes. 'And who was this young man, Irine, eh?' she asked. 'Not Costas Menelus who loves her so devotedly —I will gamble my life on it!' She used her hands in a dismissive gesture of such violence that Corinne jumped. '*Ohi, óhi*, that foolish girl would not have the sense to be with someone as dependable as Costas Menelus! She was with Takis Lemou, we may be sure of it!'

Irine knew it too, Corinne could see, but she sought to deny it because she could not bear to admit her daughter's duplicity, and it was for Irine that she felt most pity. 'She was forbidden to see him long ago, Mitéra. Not for many months has she seen him— she would not deceive her mama so!'

'She would see him!' Madame Kolianos insisted, seeing no unkindness in her persistence. 'I warned Gregori that to forbid her was of no use, but—Agh!' She dismissed her son's attempts to break up Iole's affair scornfully. 'She will follow her own way as the Kolianoses always do, and you see what her disobedience has brought her to! A hospital bed, with her mama and her *yayá* weeping for her!' She looked out of the window and frowned impatiently. '*Epiph!* Where is that chauffeur?'

It had been Gregori who spent half the night at the hospital with Irine, returning in the early hours of the morning. Madame Kolianos had stayed only a short time at the hospital, then left Irine with her daughter, but Gregori was the strong right arm that Irine needed in a crisis, and he was willing to take his brother's place when he was needed.

Quite obviously nothing had been mentioned about the baby before Madame Kolianos left, or she would never have returned home looking so blithely confident of her granddaughter's swift recovery. Perhaps Iole was managing to keep her secret, or perhaps she could not bring herself to tell anyone else but her mother at this stage. Either way it was rather like sitting on a volcano, waiting for the news to break.

But anxious or not, Corinne had become so sleepy by one o'clock in the morning that she had gone to bed and fallen asleep, despite all her efforts to stay awake. When Gregori eventually came home she had merely stirred and opened a sleepy eye, not even remembering why he had been gone so long, then turned into his arms and slept again, content to know he was there. It was not until the following morning, when she woke to find him already dressed, that she learned how closely affected she was to be.

'*Kaliméra,* my love.' Gregori came to her the moment he realised she was awake, bending to take her in his arms and hold her close while he kissed her mouth, lifting her, warm with sleep, from the pillows. 'You slept so soundly you did not even wake when I came to bed.'

'I tried to stay awake,' she confessed, and let him go only reluctantly when he gently disengaged her arms from his neck. There was something about him this morning that was subtly different, and she knew the minute her sleep-dazed brain cleared that he had learned about Iole's baby. 'You were a long time at the hospital,' she ventured. 'Is everything all right with Iole, darling?'

Sitting up in bed she could watch his reflection in the dressing-table mirror while he leaned forward and fashioned a knot in the new silk tie she had given him. And in those few moments she regretted more than ever not having told him about the baby. He was usually so amiable and good-tempered in the mornings, but today there was an air of restraint about him that she found unnerving.

He said little, but the quick impatient movements of his hands gave an indication of the stress he was under, and she watched him with growing anxiety. He had probably slept little last night, for there were shadows beneath his eyes and a downward curve to his mouth that was not usually there, and she longed to comfort him.

'She is with child!'

He made the announcement so suddenly and un-expectedly that Corinne had no time to fake her reaction. Instead of looking blankly shocked as he probably expected, she obeyed her first instinct and hastily avoided his eyes, making no verbal comment at all. Only when she saw his head come up slowly and his dark eyes narrow when they met hers briefly via the mirror did she realise too late how much she had betrayed simply by not saying or doing anything at all.

'I said that Iole is expecting a child.' He turned from the mirror and faced her, his dark eyes still narrowed. 'Are you not even a little surprised to learn that my niece is pregnant, Corinne?'

It was too late to show surprise now, so Corinne simply shook her head. 'I'm—I'm so sorry, my darling,' she said huskily. 'I know what a shock it must be for you.'

He said nothing for a moment or two, and Corinne sat with her heart thudding hard and her eyes looking anywhere but at him. It was only just dawning on her just how hurt and angry he was going to be because she had kept something as important as this from him, and she had never rued anything in her life as much as she did making that rash promise to his niece.

'When did you know?' His voice had a chill flatness that she hated and she shook her head quickly.

'Not very long, I——'

'But no one else knew!' The dark face was savage with emotion. 'Why did she not confide in those who love her? Why should she trust you with her secret? Not her mother, not me or her grandmother, but you! Why?'

He looked so tall and virile standing there at the end of the bed and she wanted so much to feel the strength of his arms around her, and the hard, relentless pressure of his kisses on her mouth, that she ached for him. She had never loved him as much as she did now, when he stood looking at her so accusingly.

'I—I found out,' she whispered.

Gregori approached the bed and she instinctively lifted herself to a more upright position and tucked her feet up under her, gasping aloud when he suddenly clamped a hand about her wrist. Bringing his face down close to hers, his eyes gleamed darkly with anger, hurt, blame, who knew what passions burned behind their fierce blackness?

'How much more have you—found out—about this sordid business?' he demanded. *Theós mou*, you know so much and say nothing to me! What kind of a wife have I married?'

'Gregori, don't, please, you have no right——'

'I have every right to be angry when my wife keeps such important matters from me!' he declared firmly. 'As Iole's guardian as well as her uncle, I have the right to protect her from her own foolishness, but how can I when such matters are kept from me by my own wife?'

'It isn't foolishness to want to choose her own husband!' Corinne argued desperately. 'You should have let her marry Takis Lemou instead of making it necessary for them to meet in secret!'

He looked down at her flushed and defiant face as if he saw someone there he had never seen before, and his eyes narrowed like chips of jet between their thick lashes. 'You are very well informed,' he said harshly, 'What else have you kept from me, Corinne, eh?'

Uneasily Corinne remembered her wedding day, when she had seen Takis Lemou coming from Iole's room, although she had not realised it at the time. But it could do no good to tell Gregori about that now and she pushed it firmly to the back of her mind.

'There's nothing else,' she denied huskily, but Gregori's expression showed how hard he found that to believe.

'You were her confidante, I suppose,' he went on in a flat bitter voice. 'Knowing that you sympathised with her, she made you her courier, did she, my scheming little wife?'

'No, never!' Corinne tugged at her wrist, looking up despairingly into that dark implacable face. 'Though I don't deny they had my sympathy!' She shook her head, her eyes bright and defensive, at once pleading and indignant. 'I would have told you, Gregori, but I'd made a promise I couldn't break. Anyway,' she added recklessly, 'I imagine you're the last person she'd want to know about it, when you've gone to so much trouble to marry her off to a man she doesn't want!'

She knew the jibe would strike home, but she regretted it almost before the words left her mouth, and for a breathless moment she thought he was going to hit her. One hand clenched and his dark eyes blazed with such fury that she instinctively shrank back. '*Theós mou*!' Gregori whispered harshly. 'You really believe I would strike you! What a monster you and Iole must think me!'

He turned and went abruptly out of the room and Corinne sank back against the pillows, feeling weak with reaction after such an emotional upheaval. Then she turned and buried her face in them suddenly, and wept. Just when she had thought everything was going so well between them, she had raised a barrier of secrecy and broken his trust in her. It must seem to him that both she and Iole found it easier to confide in a near stranger than in him, who loved them both.

Never since their marriage had she been in any doubt that she loved him, but there were so many things about him that she had to learn that sometimes she despaired of ever knowing him completely, much as she longed to. Maybe, she thought, as she hugged the pillow to her breast, she never would know him completely.

Since his abrupt departure the previous morning, Gregori's attitude had been subtly different. He was quieter and shorter in his speech, although not noticeably bad-tempered. He seemed more aloof than he had ever been, and to Corinne the difference was intolerable. She would have given anything to have things restored to the way they had been before he discovered Iole's secret, and on more than one occasion Corinne privately raged against his niece for extracting that promise from her.

'Iole's coming home tomorrow, isn't she?'

Corinne sat in front of the dressing-table mirror brushing her hair while Gregori shrugged into his jacket, and for a moment their eyes met via the mirror. 'She is,' he agreed quietly, and the abruptnesss of his tone annoyed her almost as much as it hurt. She had attempted to make her peace, and the least he could do was to meet her half-way.

One hand smoothing down her dress, she got up from the stool and walked over to him, then shook her head as she looked up into that dark, unresponsive face. 'What must I do?' she asked huskily. 'I'm truly sorry that I didn't tell you about Iole, but I promised her, and I couldn't break my promise.'

For a moment he regarded her steadily without saying anything, then he took a glance at himself in the mirror behind her and straightened his jacket. 'You once made me a promise that you would marry me,' he reminded her in a quiet, almost matter-of-fact voice, 'but you were quite prepared to break your promise until I made you change your mind.'

'That was different!' she insisted, not quite steadily,

then quite unconsciously lifted her chin a little, when rebellion stirred in her faintly. 'I suppose you've since regretted making me change my mind,' she suggested, and the dark eyes held hers steadily.

'Have you?' he countered softly, and she shook her head. 'Then why should you imagine me any more disillusioned with our marriage than you are, Corinne?'

'Maybe because you think I make a habit of deceiving you!' Her mouth trembled slightly, but when she looked up at him there was a hint of exasperation in her eyes as well as appeal. 'You're so—unbending,' she accused huskily. 'I admit I should perhaps have told you about Iole, or maybe hinted at it. But all I did was keep quiet about something I was sworn not to reveal and which you were bound to know about before very long, and you treat me as if I've committed a mortal sin! You *do*,' she insisted when something in his eyes made her pulse flutter so wildly that she put a hand to her throat in an oddly defensive gesture.

'So?' He moved a step nearer and the dark eyes looked down at her steadily, the gleam of passion in their depths arousing her own senses to respond as they always did. He placed his hands in the small of her back and pressed her close to him, then brushed his mouth across hers, lightly and temptingly, until she reached up her arms to him. 'Sometimes I think you have bewitched me,' he whispered against her lips. 'You make me angry, then you beguile me with your eyes. Oh, *Théos*, but I love you!'

His mouth was hard and fierce and the hungry urgency of his kisses left her breathless and yielding, unaware of anything but the fact that she loved him more than she had ever dreamed was possible. When he raised his head at last, she smiled at the deep dark glow in his eyes with a sense of triumphant happiness.

'I wish poor Iole could be half as happy as I am at this moment,' she whispered, and the arms that held her so tightly eased her away from him slightly while he looked down into her face. 'I believe she really loves that young man of hers, my darling, and I think she should be allowed to marry him, especially now.'

'Oh, you do?' Nothing in his eyes gave her reason to hope he was going to take a more lenient view of Iole's case, no matter how passionately he had healed the breach between the two of them. 'Do you know Takis Lemou?'

Corinne chose not to remember the few seconds when she had been face to face with that furtive young man on the landing, and shook her head. 'You know I don't,' she said.

'Exactly!' He dropped a light kiss on her brow, then eased her away from him for a second while he straightened his tie, a quite unconscious gesture that she watched with a vague feeling of irritation. 'But you think that in view of the fact that he has given her a child, she should be allowed to marry him?'

'Oh, darling, *yes*, if she loves him!'

She felt strangely bereft without his arms around her, and she put her hands on her own arms for a moment to simulate his warmth, while she tried to see his point of view. Gregori watched her for a second or two and heaven knew what was going on behind those deep unfathomable eyes, then he bent his head and kissed her mouth with a lingering slowness.

'You are too blinded by romantic happy endings, my love,' he told her. 'They do not always happen. Any man may father a child, but he will not always make a good husband. Takis Lemou would not!'

'Obviously Iole believes he would,' Corinne told him, and he put a finger over her lips as he turned to go.

'Then it is as well that my opinion counts for more,' he said.

He left her to make her way down to breakfast with the others, at the long table in the garden. The morning air always smelled so wonderful with the clean freshness of pine mingling with the rest of the delicious scents that the perfumed garden provided, but she always missed Gregori at breakfast-time.

He was usually gone before the rest of them had finished their meals and Corinne still felt a certain reticence when she was alone with his family. Madame Kolianos and Irine both treated her with perfect courtesy, and if Zoe sometimes injected a little malice into her conversation, she always declared it quite unintentional.

When Corinne joined them she found that the conversation was, almost inevitably, centred on Iole. Apparently Costas Menelus had asked to be allowed to see her in hospital and, although Irine was obviously in some doubt as to the wisdom of it, Gregori had insisted that he be allowed to see her; and as usual his argument prevailed.

'My son is a great believer in the power of love,' his mother observed with a hint of irony. 'But no matter how much young Costas declares himself in love with Iole, I cannot believe that Stefan Menelus will allow him to marry her!' Catching sight of Irine's expression suddenly, she reached over and patted her hand. 'We shall need to love and support that foolish child in the months to come, more than ever before,' she said.

Corinne, to whom the solution was obvious, felt a sense of exasperation that none of them seemed to have mentioned it yet. 'Isn't she going to marry—Takis

Lemou?' she asked. 'Surely no one can refuse her now?'

The silence was uneasy and she could sense the exchange of glances between the two older women, just as she was aware, rather unexpectedly, of Zoe's smile of approval. When she looked up at her she saw a curious glitter in her eyes which she found oddly disturbing and hastily avoided.

'It might happen!' Zoe said, then laughed in a way that brought a swift frown to Madame Kolianos's black brows. 'With a little help from the right people.' She gazed at Corinne so intently that she was eventually bound to look at her again, and she quizzed her with arched brows when she did so. 'Do you think it is possible, Corinne?'

'I—I don't know.'

She was too unsure just what answer her bright, defiant sister-in-law was after and she went on buttering a roll, with her mind only half on the job she was doing. 'Gregori adores her,' Zoe mused, as if speculating on just how much. 'And Iole knows it—it could well be that she counted on his loving her enough to consent.'

It took several moments for the full meaning of what she said to dawn on her listeners, and when it did Corinne stared at her doubtfully. Madame Kolianos, however, put her view more forcefully, and yet something in her expression suggested that she did not entirely dismiss the idea out of hand.

'I do not like your meaning, Zoe,' she told her daughter sharply. 'Iole is an intelligent child and she would not take such a foolish risk!'

'You cannot believe that, Zoe,' said Irine, but her gentle face showed signs of uncertainty as she considered the perfumed garden provided, but she always missed risky form of emotional blackmail to gain her own ends.

Obviously it was something she could not accept and she shook her head firmly. 'It is a most disgraceful thing to suggest!' she told Zoe, who seemed undeterred by anyone's opinion.

'Would you blame her?' she challenged swiftly. 'If it was the only way she had of gaining Gregori's and your consent to marry Takis Lemou?'

'It would be wicked,' Madame Kolianos decreed. 'And although Iole is certainly foolish, she is not wicked; I will not believe that she is wicked.'

'No, Mama.'

Madame Kolianos looked at her daughter sternly. She seldom scolded Zoe, the child born to her in her later years and the joy of her life as well as the source of most of her anger. Zoe was spoiled and revelled in it, but in this instance she had earned a reprimand and she would get it.

'There will be no more said on this matter,' Madame Kolianos decreed. 'It is for Irine to decide what shall happen to her child.'

'And Gregori,' Zoe murmured irrepressibly, but fell silent when her mother frowned warningly. 'Yes, Mama.'

The subject was dropped as Madame Kolianos decreed, but the rest of the meal was eaten in a rather uneasy silence, and the moment Corinne left the table Zoe hastily excused herself and came hurrying after her. It was unusual enough for Zoe to seek her company to make Corinne look at her curiously from the corner of her eye as they went upstairs together.

Only when they had walked half the length of the landing and stood outside Zoe's bedroom door did the purpose of her uncharacteristic move become clear. She stood for a moment with a hand on the door knob, regarding Corinne with one of her faintly quizzical smiles.

'Do you really care about Iole?' she asked, and the question came as such a surprise that for a moment or two Corinne simply stared at her.

'Well, of course I do,' she said after a while, and felt uneasily suspicious of Zoe's motives suddenly. 'What are you getting at, Zoe?'

Zoe looked briefly puzzled by the colloquialism, then eyed her steadily with a bright gleam of challenge in her dark eyes. 'If you were to beg Gregori to let her marry Takis Lemou,' she said, 'maybe he would relent.'

To Corinne the idea of ever raising that particular subject again with her husband was out of the question, and she shook her head even before Zoe had finished speaking. 'I couldn't,' she told her. 'And it wouldn't do any good, Zoe. I've already tried and failed!'

For a moment the girl's dark eyes studied her narrowly, discomfitingly reminiscent of her brother's, then she laughed shortly and pursed her lower lip. 'A new bride?' she questioned softly. 'Have you no influence over your husband, Corinne? Surely a few soft words, a little— persuasion, hmm? Surely a bride for whom he fought so determinedly has sufficient influence over her man to make him see that others should be allowed their free choice of a marriage partner also? If he truly loves you, he will not refuse you.'

She was being goaded, and Corinne knew it, but she would not risk further quarrels with Gregori for Iole or anyone else. No matter how she sympathised with his niece, she was not going to run any risks with her own marriage, and she shook her head firmly.

'Zoe, for Iole's sake I wish it was possible, but it isn't, I know it isn't. He won't listen to me where Iole's concerned, and I daren't——' She corrected herself hastily. 'I'd rather not make it too much of an issue between us at the moment.'

Zoe's eyes below arched black brows gleamed at her mockingly. 'You are afraid of making him angry?' she asked.

'Not afraid, no,' Corinne denied swiftly, 'but I'd rather not quarrel with him over something that isn't really my business.'

'Not even though you claim to care for Iole?' Clearly Zoe had a very poor opinion of her and Corinne hated to have to admit that no matter how he claimed to love her, or how eagerly he had made up their brief quarrel, she did not believe Gregori would listen to any further argument on the subject of his niece. 'Perhaps,' Zoe went on in her smooth quiet voice, 'you do not have very much influence with my brother? In the circumstances it is understandable——'

She shrugged and was about to turn into her room, but Corinne put a staying hand on her arm, troubled by something she was not yet sure of. 'What do you mean, Zoe—in the circumstances?'

The dark eyes were steady but not quite direct. 'Has he not told you about Persephone?' Zoe asked softly. 'Has he not been—honest?'

The thudding beat of Corinne's heart almost choked her, for she could recall a time when Irine had been, so she believed, evasive about whether or not Gregori had ever been close to being married before; and Irine was not normally evasive. 'You said—Persephone?' Her own voice had a whispering harshness.

Zoe's eyes shifted, but not before they had seen the look on Corinne's face. 'I do not think I should say any more about her,' she said. 'If Gregori had wanted you to know he would have told you himself, although it would not be easy for him.'

'Zoe!' Corinne's fingers closed hard over Zoe's arm

and prevented her from leaving her as she sought to. 'I want to know about Persephone! And since you've taken the trouble to mention her to me, *you* can tell me!'

'Are you jealous?' Her eyes speculated on the possibility, and her full mouth twisted into a tight smile. 'Oh, you have no need to be, Corinne, for she is married! How we all wish she was *not*!' she added, and sighed. 'What a bride she would have made for Gregori, and how happy he would have been! Persephone could have persuaded him to do anything.'

'Who *was* she, Zoe!'

'*Is*,' Zoe corrected her with relentless accuracy. 'Like Iole, her family would not let her break her betrothal to marry the man she loves and who loves her. Oh, she is so beautiful—cultured, wealthy, charming and passionate; everything a man like Gregori wants and needs, especially when he knows he cannot have her. No wonder he could not bear to marry another Greek woman—a Greek would have reminded him constantly of Persephone! Would you not think,' Zoe mused, 'that having suffered himself he would show more compassion for Iole? But no! He does not deserve to be happy!'

Persephone! The name raced round and round in Corinne's head and for a moment she felt physically sick. Just thinking of Gregori wishing day after day that he could have married another woman, having her always in his mind——

'But he loves *me*!' She said it aloud, shrill in her anguish, and she realised that Zoe only now recognised how deeply she had hurt. To impress it on her own mind she repeated it. 'He loves *me*, he's said so many times that he loves me!'

Zoe used her hands, spreading them wide and refusing to meet her eyes. She opened her bedroom door and this time Corinne made no move to keep her. 'It is possible that he does,' she allowed. 'In a way, he loves you.' But Corinne scarcely heard her, her whole world seemed suddenly to have been turned upside down. 'Because he cannot have Persephone, and he needs to love someone.'

CHAPTER SEVEN

CORINNE wished with all her heart that she could forget what Zoe had told her, but she found it impossible. Something in Zoe's manner suggested that she was telling the truth, although possibly exaggerating a little, and the memory of it nagged Corinne unrelentingly as she lay there in the darkness.

To make matters worse, when Gregori had tried to coax her into the loving mood she was usually so willing to enjoy, she had found it impossible to be as responsive as she normally was, and for the first time he had turned from her, puzzled and angry, but yielding to her obvious unwillingness. Now, instead of being cradled in his arms, she gazed up at the shadowy ceiling, trying to forget the woman whom Zoe claimed he loved; whom he had always loved.

She knew nothing about her, other than that she was rich, beautiful and married, but as the night lengthened she began to hate the conjured-up vision of a classical Greek beauty with an intensity that startled her. When she had hesitated about coming to Greece in the first place, Robert had tried to persuade her to let Gregori take second-best as he called it, and marry someone more acceptable to his family. Suddenly discovering that *she* was second-best was a bitter pill indeed to swallow, and she brushed an impatient hand across her eyes when she realised there were tears in them.

The movement, however slight, must have disturbed Gregori, for he turned towards her and she felt her flesh tingle when she sensed him watching her in the soft darkness of the moonlit room. But when a tentative hand reached over and touched her she flinched from it and turned her head away. 'Corinne?' Her body ached to respond to that soft-voiced enquiry, but she found it too easy to imagine that in the darkness he pretended to himself that she was Persephone, his real love, and she kept her head turned away from him.

Murmuring something softly in Greek, he moved the familiar warmth of his body nearer, pressing close against her and arousing her senses while she fought to subdue them. While she tried to drown them in what she saw as righteous anger at his deception. Maybe she could have forgiven him if he had told her, but to remember how he had snatched her from Robert and made such a fuss about her friendship with him, made her angry as well as hurt.

A hand on her cheek turned her gently to face him. 'My love,' he whispered, 'what is the matter, eh?' Corinne stayed silent, unable to speak without screaming at him that his love for another woman was the matter, and he raised himself slightly so that he looked down into her face, his mouth only a breath away and already brushing softly against her lips. '*Agapitikós*, please tell me what is troubling you. Why do you turn away from me?'

A light kiss tempted her to yield, but Corinne tried once more to turn her head away, and the sudden fierce pressure of his mouth was a determined effort to prevent it, like the strong fingers that curved into her cheek. Unable to help herself, she yielded for just a moment to the clamour of her senses, but the persistent ghost that Zoe had raised once more hovered between them and she jerked her head aside, breathing hard, and angry because there were tears still in her eyes.

Gregori was growing angry too, she could feel the tautness of the lean body beside her and the tightening of his hands. But the shadow of his beautiful Persephone loomed too large now to be dismissed, and the name was torn from her as she spun over on to her side and turned her back to him, her voice muffled and unsteady.

'Persephone! Who is Persephone?'

To Corinne his very silence seemed to confirm her worst fears, but he remained as he was in the taut, quiet seconds that followed. Just out of touch but close enough to make her aware of his nearness and the turbulence of his mood.

'She is someone I have known for a very long time—someone we have all known for a long time.' His deep quiet voice was well under control as it always was. 'Why do you ask, Corinne? Why do you question me about her now, in the small hours of the morning?'

'But who *is* she?'

In her desperation her voice was a strangled whisper, and Gregori was silent once more for several seconds before he answered. When he did his voice was still perfectly controlled; quiet as the hour demanded, but controlled. 'If you wish to know her name it is Persephone Chambi, but why should she concern you? And particularly at this moment!' He gripped her hard suddenly and pulled her back to face him, holding her with bruising force while she struggled in vain to be free. In the diffused moonlight his eyes glittered darkly and she turned her head back and forth to try and shut out the hovering shadow of his face. 'Why, Corinne?'

'I want to sleep,' she panted breathlessly. 'Let me go, you can't——'

'I am entitled to know why my wife suddenly behaves as if she finds my lovemaking repellent to her,' he insisted remorselessly. 'And why she chooses the small hours of the morning to question me about another woman!'

'Why didn't you tell me about her?'

She made the demand in a harsh whisper, for she was almost out of breath. She had given up struggling against him, but she tried to cope with such a tangle of emotions that her head was spinning. She loved him and she desperately wanted him to love her, but not if he saw her only as second best to a woman he had loved even before he knew her. Whom he still loved, according to Zoe.

'Why should I tell you about her?' Gregori asked, and the quietness of his voice contrasted so strongly with the physical passion she knew possessed his body that she shuddered. 'There is nothing you need to know; nothing that need concern you. I owe you no excuses, no explanations—and certainly not at this hour!'

'I'm only your wife!' She sounded so bitter that Gregori frowned.

'You would do well to remember it, *kopéla mou*!'

'Is that what you mean to do?' Corinne whispered. 'Remind me that I'm your wife and you need me, even though you're lusting after another man's wife!'

'You *dare* to say that!'

He resorted to his own tongue as he most often did in moments of stress, and lying there in the half-dark with

him Corinne trembled, half afraid of the fury she had un-
leashed. With his strong fingers Gregori pressed her
hands into the pillows, pinning her body down with
the broad, bronze smoothness of his chest. Every dark
contour of his face was deepened and intensified by the
shadowy light, and she could not tear her eyes away from
it.

'I married *you*!' he rasped in a voice that sent shudders
through her trembling body. 'You are *my* wife and that is
all that concerns me; it is all that should concern you!'

Her eyes had a shimmering mistiness as she looked up
into that mask of darkness hovering over her, and the
lateness of the hour as well as the turmoil of her emotions
had taken their toll. As she lay there sleepless, Zoe's
words had come back to her again and again, growing in
importance until the desire to be revenged on that
shadowy lover he coveted and could not have was a very
real and urgent need.

'I thought it was all that mattered,' she whispered, 'but
I can't make love with a man who sees me only as a
substitute for a woman he can't have!'

He said something in his own tongue, bringing his face
with its gleaming dark eyes closer to hers. His mouth
touched hers, just lightly for a second and then suddenly
with more force, as he sought to arouse her usual response. When she lay there determinedly unresponsive
and with tears pricking her eyes, he kissed her again; a
fierce, violent kiss, using not just his mouth but his whole
body.

'We shall see what you will do, my love!' he whispered
harshly. 'We shall see!'

Gregori left for the office rather earlier than usual the
following morning, and rather than risk questions about

her behaviour last night, Corinne feigned sleep. By morning the question of Persephone Chambi seemed to have taken on more reasonable proportions; maybe Zoe had, if not actually lied, at least exaggerated Gregori's interest in the woman.

Corinne was not naïve enough to suppose that a man of Gregori's temperament had lived for thirty-five years without having known a fair number of women, some of them probably quite intimately. Maybe Persephone Chambi had been an affair that had lasted for longer than most. Nevertheless, rather than have the matter raised again this morning, she had deliberately curled herself over on to her side and kept her eyes tightly shut.

She so very nearly betrayed herself, though, when Gregori bent and gently kissed the side of her neck, brushing aside a tumble of auburn hair to do it, for she was tempted to turn and kiss him as she would normally have done. Instead, the memory of last night, when he had forcibly demanded of her what she usually gave so willingly, kept her stubbornly inert, and only when he had quietly left her did she turn and gaze thoughtfully at the closed door.

She breakfasted in near silence and was so preoccupied that Madame Kolianos commented upon it. Just as later the same day her mother-in-law's shrewd dark eyes watched her from across the room when she received a telephone call.

'It is a man, but not Gregori,' Zoe told her, and a gleam in her eyes mocked Corinne's puzzled frown. 'Perhaps you would prefer to use the telephone in the hall?'

Clearly Zoe was just as sure as Corinne herself who the caller was, and knowing the speculation it must be causing she set her chin at a defiant angle when she did as Zoe suggested and took it in the hall. 'Hello, Robert?'

'Yes, it's me, Corinne.' He sounded rather unsure of himself. 'I hope I didn't put my foot in it by asking for you.'

'Of course you didn't!' She dismissed the possibility lightly. 'I'd forgotten for the moment that you were still in Greece. Are you enjoying your long holiday?'

She felt a little mean for sounding so offhand, especially when he hesitated for a moment, for she could too easily imagine his rather earnest face looking downcast and disappointed. 'Not as much as I might have done,' he told her. 'But I love the place and the people; they're not all as inhospitable as your Greek, I'm glad to say!' He laughed a little awkwardly, going on before she could answer him. 'I'm sorry, love! What I really rang for was to see how you're getting on; is married life suiting you?'

In the circumstances it was a difficult question to answer, but not for anything would Corinne have let him know that things were anything other than perfect between her and Gregori at the moment, and she laughed. 'Fine, thank you, Robert.'

But Robert had known her for a long time and it was almost as if he detected something behind her laughter. 'I just wondered,' he went on after a second or two, 'if it would be possible for me to see you again. I'm writing to my folks and I'd like to be able to tell them that I've seen you and that you're looking as beautiful as ever and in blooming health. I'd like to see for myself.'

'I've written to Ann and Clifford,' Corinne told him, playing for time before she gave him an answer he was not going to like. 'I've written twice, as a matter of fact, and——'

'You needn't worry, I haven't told them anything about the—the differences I've had with your lord and master,' Robert told her dryly. 'I said I saw you on the day you were married and that you looked out of this world, that's all. But—couldn't you see me for just a minute or two, Corinne?'

Corinne hesitated. It was a long time since she had last seen him, on the day she was married, and she could not pretend that in other circumstances she would have agreed without stopping to think. But Gregori had been adamant and she was reluctant to make matters any worse between them at the moment. 'I'm sorry, Robert.' Her voice must have told him how reluctant she was to refuse. 'But I don't think it would be a very good idea at the moment. I know it's been a while now, but Gregori was quite adamant——'

'What have you married there?' Robert demanded. 'A full-blooded tyrant? He hasn't still got you on a leash, has he? What does he do—lock you up each day before he leaves for the office?'

'You're being offensive, Robert!' Her defence of Gregori was instinctive and automatic and she could sense Robert's surprise, so that she made an immediate attempt to appease him. 'Maybe I could meet you for a coffee one day : you don't go back just yet, do you?'

'Very soon,' he told her. 'I wish you'd make the effort, love, I've been very disappointed at not seeing you at all when you were the main reason I scratched together all this leave.'

'I know, Robert, and I'm truly sorry it worked out as it did, but—well, you did rather make a rod for your own back by being so aggressive each time you and Gregori met, didn't you?' She did not wait for his reply, but hurried on. 'There's been a bit of family upheaval lately, so I'd rather not commit myself right off, but later——'

'O.K.' She heard his resigned sigh and could imagine the slight stoop of his shoulders that always betrayed his disappointment. 'But believe me, I've no intention of leaving for home without seeing you again, you can tell your arrogant Greek that!'

'I promise I'll see you before you leave.' She could see no alternative but to make him the promise, and even Gregori could not be so unreasonable as to forbid her to say goodbye to Robert. 'Actually I've written and told your folks; Gregori has to go to England at the end of the year and he's promised to take me with him. So I shall be seeing you all then.'

'Nice of him!' Robert declared tartly. 'Can I ring you there when I want to let you know I'm leaving?'

Corinne hesitated. There was no point in preventing him calling and she was not, as Robert suggested, a prisoner even though Gregori would probably be furious if he knew about this call. 'I don't see why not,' she told Robert. 'But your little fisherman's cottage doesn't have a phone, does it?'

'I'm in the *taverna* on the quay,' Robert informed her. 'Nikos Thelassi has the only telephone on the island and I have an audience.'

She heard a shout go up behind him and she could visualise the spartan comfort of the tiny *taverna* with its all male customers. Robert had settled so well into the life of an islander that it was a pity he could not have got on as well with her particular Greek. Not that anyone could remain aloof for very long from the determined hospitality of the Greek islanders.

'Let me know when you're leaving,' she told him, 'and we'll arrange something.'

'Oh well, I suppose half a loaf is better than no bread at all,' Robert quoted ruefully. 'I'll have to be content with the prospect of at least being able to say goodbye to you.'

'I'm sorry.'

There seemed little else she could say, and Corinne felt strangely in need of a friendly face while she was at odds with Gregori. It would have been nice to see Robert again, but she was not taking any chances. For a second or two there was nothing at the other end of the line but the faint buzz of voices in the background, and then Robert spoke again, his mouth obviously very close to the instrument and his voice kept low so as not to be overheard.

'I love you, Corinne!'

The line went dead almost at once and she stood for a moment staring at the telephone and not quite sure why she felt so suddenly tearful. It was curious how she had always taken Robert for granted until the day he drove her to the airport to catch the plane to Greece. Probably being married to Robert would have been much less emotionally traumatic, but she doubted if she would have known so many wildly exciting moments as she had with Gregori. And she clung to those memories like a lifeline as she replaced the receiver.

Iole was home. Looking slightly pale and with a large bruise on her chin, but none the worse otherwise, and Corinne considered that both she and her companion in the car had been very fortunate to get off as lightly as they had. She looked so young that Corinne's heart went out to her, and she wondered what was going to happen to her now that marriage to Costas Menelus was almost certainly out of the question.

Irine had told her that Costas had worshipped Iole ever since he was a schoolboy—he was only nineteen now—and at one time Iole had seemed of the same mind about him. Only the advent of Takis Lemou, older and more confident of his prowess as a ladies' man, had made her change her mind, but Costas had never changed his. If it was at all possible for him to marry Iole, even now, she believed he still would.

Corinne looked across at Iole now and wondered if she was as troubled by her uncertain future as Irine was. Since she came home she had been treated with a gentle consideration and not one word of reproach, but it was quite evident to Corinne that she was under constant supervision from one or another member of the family. Whether Iole herself realised it, she could not tell, but if she did she showed no sign that it troubled her.

Now that she was more at home in her new country, Corinne sometimes went shopping alone and this morning she was tempted to ask if Iole would like to come with her, for the change of scene. What stopped her offering was the possibility that Iole might be nervous about riding in a car after the accident, otherwise she might have enjoyed her company.

Corinne still felt curiously awkward whenever she used the chauffeur-driven car, although Gregori had mocked her for it. 'Kiría Corinne Kolianos rides in a limousine, my lark,' he had told her with a laugh. 'She does not need to use public transport.' Yet sometimes Corinne felt she would have felt more at home travelling by bus.

'I'm off now,' she said as she got to her feet. 'Is there anything I can bring for anyone while I'm out?'

The offer was declined with a murmur of thanks, but when she was only half-way across the hall she realised someone else had left the room after her and was trying to catch up. Turning curiously, she saw Iole and smiled, noticing how the girl glanced back over her shoulder before she spoke.

'Are you driving into Piraeus, Corinne?' she asked, and

made such an obvious effort to keep her voice inaudible to those left in the salon that Corinne felt vaguely uneasy. Nevertheless she nodded agreement.

'I thought it would make a change from Athens,' she told her. 'Why, Iole? Is there something I can bring for you after all?'

From the way she hesitated it was clear that Iole was in some doubt about the request she had to make and her eyes were too evasive for Corinne's peace of mind. 'Will you do a service for me?' she asked.

Suspicious suddenly, Corinne eyed her doubtfully. A pulse in her throat fluttered warningly as she watched the defiant yet undeniably anxious young face, and she put her question with obvious caution. 'What is it you want me to do, Iole?'

'To deliver a message, that is all.'

Corinne's heart thudded at her ribs while she hesitated, and yet something in that young face appealed to her soft heart and she went on instead of refusing out of hand, as would probably have been wiser. 'To Takis Lemou?' she asked, and Iole nodded.

'I would not ask it of you,' she promised, flicking a pointed tongue over her lips, 'but I cannot ask Zoe since Thíos Gregori has discovered that she helped me before.'

'Zoe did?' It should not have come as such a surprise, but somehow it did. Her sister-in law, it seemed, took a very active interest in all her family's love affairs. 'I didn't know that.'

'But she can no longer help me and I *must* send Takis a message! Please, Corinne!'

The plea was in such earnest and the young voice so plaintively unsteady that Corinne found it much too hard to refuse. Heaven knew, the past few days had been nerve-racking enough for Iole and, although she had the comfort and solace of her home and family, her future still hung in the balance. A future without the man she loved, unless someone helped her. It was a sentimental situation that was bound to appeal to Corinne, and in all probability Iole was aware of it.

'I should refuse outright,' she told Iole, and shook her head over her own weakness, 'but if I do take this message for you, I want you to promise that Gregori will never hear of it.'

'Oh yes, yes, I promise!'

Seeing herself as committed, Corinne sighed inwardly. 'Where do I find him?' she asked. 'Do I have to go to his home? Or simply post a letter to him?'

Iole's eyes were evasive again, sliding away when Corinne tried to look at her. 'His family do not know of our association,' she confessed with a hint of her usual defiance. She took an envelope from the pocket of her dress and handed it to her. 'You will find him in a *cafenion* just off the waterfront,' she said, and gave her such precise instructions how to get there that it was obvious she had been there herself. 'He meets there with his friends.'

'I see.' Corinne recalled the exclusively masculine clientele of the average Greek coffee shop, and looked doubtful.

'Oh, no one will take notice of a foreign woman going in there,' Iole assured her without for a moment sounding as if she used the term offensively. 'Please do this for me, Corinne. I have not seen or heard of Takis since I came from the hospital and I must—I must know——'

'Yes, of course you must!' Corinne concealed her misgivings and tried to put Iole's mind at rest. 'I promise not to let you down, Iole; the question is, how do I know this boy-friend of yours?'

For a moment Iole's eyes had that oblique and slightly sly look of old. 'You saw him once; on your wedding day, do you not remember?' she asked, then had the grace to look ashamed because Corinne's expression reminded her of her deception on that occasion.

'I remember the incident,' she said, 'but I'm afraid I can't remember what he looked like.'

'Like this!' Once more Iole plunged a hand into the pocket of her dress and this time produced a photograph, slightly crumpled and with lipstick traces on the face of it. 'Only please,' she begged with touching anxiety, 'let me have it back, Corinne, because it is the only one I have of him. He is handsome, no?'

'Very,' Corinne agreed, and wondered how anyone but a rather foolish and impulsive girl like Iole could be taken in by Takis Lemou's flashy good looks. If she could have done so without appearing completely heartless and breaking her promise, she would have changed her mind. As it was she kept her opinion to herself. 'I'll see what I can do, Iole,' she promised.

'Oh, thank you!' For a moment Iole stood there, obviously with something on her mind that was not easy to put into words, and the look in her eyes was vaguely defensive when she eventually spoke. 'I am pleased that Thíos Gregori has married you!' she said in a light breathless voice, then turned and walked back to the salon.

It was one of the times when Corinne wished she had learned to drive or that she could have taken a bus instead of the chauffeur-driven car that she was expected to use. As it was she took the precaution of leaving the car some distance from her eventual destination and walked through the maze of small streets behind the waterfront, looking for the *cafénion* that Iole had told her about.

But finding it was the least of her problems. As she had feared, the customers were exclusively male and when she appeared in the doorway the buzz of conversation almost ceased and several games of backgammon were suspended while the participants eyed her curiously. Then someone said something that evidently amused the rest, for there was a spontaneous burst of laughter that was the final straw as far as Corinne was concerned.

She had already turned to go, her courage failing her, when she caught sight of the man she sought and hesitated. Of medium height and with curling black hair, he sat at one of the small tables in the company of four other young men, the inevitable cups of thick black coffee and accompanying glasses of water in front of them. Corinne had no need of the photograph to identify him, but for the first time she could understand the seemingly heartless ban on Iole's association with him.

For a reputedly wealthy young man he appeared to have remarkably poor taste both in his choice of companions and his surroundings. He registered her recognition of him with a swiftly arched brow and got to his feet, slowly and with an insolent awareness of his own virility, coming across the crowded café to her with a kind of lazy swagger, his eyes on her the whole time.

Feeling slightly mesmerised by the situation she found herself in. Corinne fumbled for the envelope she had brought, anxious to have it delivered and take her departure. 'I've brought a letter from Iole,' she said, speaking quickly and breathlessly, and only then stopped to wonder if he spoke English.

'So?' He drawled the word while glancing back at his companions, who grinned broadly, drawing their attention to the fact that it was he that the pretty foreigner had sought out. 'Do not go,' he begged, when Corinne would have turned away, and put a hand on her arm. 'What is your name?'

'My name doesn't matter, Mr Lemou.' Her voice was as firm as she could make it and Corinne pulled back her arm from the touch of an unpleasantly moist palm. 'I'm simply delivering Iole's letter. She's much better,' she added, for despite appearances he might be a little concerned about her.

But he laughed. 'Of course,' he said in a strong accent that was probably very popular with most foreign girls. He turned the letter over in his hand but made no attempt to open it. 'What is this about, eh?'

Thinking to shame him into being more concerned, Corinne looked him in the eye and spoke far more boldly than she would normally have done in such circumstances. 'I imagine it's about your future,' she told him. 'Yours and Iole's—why don't you read it?'

'No need!' He thrust the envelope carelessly into a pocket and fixed her with his bold eyes once more. 'I know my future well enough, *thespinís*.' He noticed the ring on her finger then and pursed his lips in a mock moue of disappointment before he laughed. '*Kiría*,' he corrected himself. 'Perhaps you are the bride of Gregori Kolianos—ah, *né*, I remember! You were the beautiful bride I saw on your wedding day when I was leaving Iole's room, *né*?' Once more his harsh laughter mocked her and he stood with his hands in his pockets, eyeing her boldly. 'You may tell your husband, Kiría Kolianos, that he need fear my intentions no longer. My friends are here to wish me *kaló taksithi*—I am flying to my uncle in America tonight!'

Corinne stared at him, leaning carelessly against the

wall and regarding her dismay with obvious amusement, but with no sign of regret or concern about Iole. 'But you —you *can't*!' She found her voice eventually, but it was small and very unsteady. 'What about Iole—and the baby? *Your* baby?'

'So?' The maddening brows kicked upward yet again and he was still smiling as if the whole situation afforded him nothing but amusement. 'There is always Costas Menelus—there is *always* Costas Menelus!'

With his laughter, Corinne realised bitterly, went the last shred of hope for Iole's precious love affair; the affair she had risked so much for, and her anger almost boiled over into verbal abuse. It was only the certain knowledge that Takis Lemou would find that also a cause for laughter that kept her silent, although she shook with anger.

The place seemed unbearably hot suddenly. She felt prickly with the heat and her head was swimming; all she could think of was finding Gregori and telling him, for she could not face Iole herself with the news that her precious Takis was about to abandon her as callously as if she was a worn-out shoe. Turning quickly, she walked once more out into the shadowy narrowness of the street, and headed back to where she had left the car.

The chauffeur looked at her curiously when she asked to be taken to the offices of the Kolianos Shipping Company, but only minutes later he stopped the car outside a tall block of offices and opened the door for her. She refused his offer to enquire if Kírios Kolianos was free, and made her own way into the small reception hall.

It was not until she was inside that she realised she would first have to confess to acting as Iole's messenger. Gregori would be angry, she had no doubt of it, but it was a risk she had to take if she was not to be the one to carry the news that Iole's whole world was about to collapse about her.

There was a lift immediately facing her as she came in the door, and a flight of stairs disappeared out of her sight to the right. Just inside the door were one or two chairs, apparently for waiting interviewees, and she could just see the corner of a desk around the right-hand corner which presumably was where she would find a receptionist. She was still getting her bearings when she heard a familiar deep, soft voice speaking in Greek, and stepped forward into the main part of the reception hall.

Gregori was coming from one of a row of doors beyond the receptionist's desk and he was for the moment unaware of her. He walked with a hand under the arm of a tall, dark woman and his head was bent slightly, as though to catch what she was saying. He was smiling, and the moment Corinne caught sight of the smoothly beautiful face of his companion she had no doubt who she was looking at.

Her first instinct was one of stunned surprise, of shock almost, because the morning's events had dimmed and diminished the importance of Persephone Chambi. To see Gregori with this undeniably lovely woman whom she had no doubt at all was the woman who had caused her such unhappiness recently was like being struck a physical blow.

Rooted to the spot with her heart thudding like the slow hard beat of a drum, she watched them come nearer, and could do nothing but watch as if she was mesmerised. Gregori's whole attention was concentrated on the oval face with its smiling mouth and lustrous dark eyes, and yet it was only a matter of seconds before he seemed to sense Corinne's presence and looked up suddenly.

She caught her breath and only just managed to keep

back the tears that threatened to blot out the sight of the two of them together. She had already been shocked enough by the prospect of Iole's heartbreak, but she had not foreseen herself being in the same position when she came to seek Gregori's help.

'Corinne! *Agapiménos*! What are you doing here?'

He was just as he always was, smiling and pleased to see her, his hands outstretched to take hers, his strong fingers caressing and soothing as he bent to kiss her. It was as if the whispered anger and violent passion of that night had never been. As if it did not matter to him that she had seen him engrossed in the company of the woman who had caused it. But that suggested a man without thought or sensitivity, and she knew that wasn't so.

'What has brought you here to see me, eh?' he asked, then put a hand beneath her chin and raised her face, looking down into it for a moment. 'Oh, my love, what has happened that you run to me with tears in your eyes?'

Reminding herself that her immediate concern was Iole, Corinne still tried to cope with her own emotions. So far she had avoided looking at the woman with him and instead kept her eyes downcast, her heavy lashes hiding the threatening tears; except from Gregori.

'I—I had to see you about something,' she said, and despaired of the way her voice trembled. 'It's rather important or I wouldn't have come. That is, I thought, if I came to you——'

'But of course you would come to me, my love, when you are so distressed! Who else would you turn to?' His fingers stroking her cheek sought to soothe her misery without knowing he was the cause of it, while dark eyes searched her face anxiously. 'Come, we will talk in my office, eh?'

Corinne made herself look at the other woman at last. Tall and elegantly coiffured, wearing clothes that flattered her somewhat full figure, she stood by, obviously interested, yet discreetly apart. Dark eyes between thick lashes looked quite unexpectedly kind and friendly as well as curious. It was the hardest thing she had ever had to do, but Corinne managed to control her feelings sufficiently to offer a conventional way out.

'If you're busy, Gregori, I could——'

'No, no, no! You will come with me now,' Gregori insisted, and was apparently still unperturbed by the situation. 'You will tell me what it is that troubles you so much, my little one.' He placed a comforting arm about her shoulders and lightly kissed her brow. 'But first I would like you to meet——'

'Persephone Chambi—who else!'

The name was out, sharp and angry, before she could stop it and the woman's fine dark brow registered surprise, while Gregori's frowned. It was a second or two before she realised that she was being offered a long slim hand to shake, and she hastily made the appropriate response, with Gregori's eyes on her, slightly narrowed in the way she knew so well.

'Persephone, as you know, is an old friend,' he said, coolly ignoring that impulsive remark. 'Persephone, I would like to introduce my wife, Corinne.'

'I am most pleased to meet you, Kiría Kolianos.' The soft smooth voice was yet another attractive feature of this secret love of her husband's, Corinne noted, and swallowed hard on the bitterness that rose in her throat like gall. 'Do you like our country—your new country?' The hasty correction was smoothly glossed over. 'I am sure you will be happy here.'

'She is already happy, are you not, my lark?' Gregori

asked, and bent to kiss her lowered lids. 'Although perhaps not at this moment, hmm?'

'But of course,' Persephone Chambi interposed smoothly. 'I will not keep you any longer, Gregori, when your wife has such need of you.' The dark eyes glanced at him meaningly. 'You will tell your wife about——'

'I will tell her in time,' Gregori interrupted her swiftly, and was obviously anxious that she should not give away whatever she had been going to mention.

Corinne looked up in time to see him shaking his head at her, and Persephone pulled a rueful face. 'Yes, of course, I am sorry.' Once more a hand was proffered for her to shake, and Corinne steeled herself to take it. 'Goodbye, Kiría Kolianos, I hope we may meet again in happier circumstances. *Hárika polí.*'

'Goodbye, Persephone.' He leaned across and kissed the round smooth cheek, and Corinne squirmed inwardly at the look the two of them exchanged. A small secret smile and a slight nod, as if of reassurance. '*Efharistó,*' he murmured, and she dared not think what he could be thanking her for.

Hugging Corinne close to his side with his arm still around her shoulders, he took her across the reception hall and into the office he had just left with Persephone. Her perfume still lingered faintly and Corinne wrinkled her nose in dislike at the reminder. The room was sparsely furnished but had the same air of simple luxury as the salon at home, and he saw her seated in a huge armchair before perching on the edge of the desk.

'That is most comfortable,' he assured her with a half-smile, then reached for a cigarette.

His hands, she noticed when he applied the flame, were perfectly steady. Apparently even being caught with his lover could not disturb that perfect self-control of his, and for a moment Corinne almost hated him. Looking down at her through the drift of smoke, he spoke quietly and coolly, holding one of her hands as he did so; a comfort she accepted gladly even feeling as she did. Somehow her own emotions had become tangled with Iole's, and she was no longer sure which of them she felt sorriest for.

'You must be very upset about whatever it is, my love,' he said, 'to show that extraordinary display of temperament just now.' He did not raise his voice, nor did he accuse, but the set of his mouth was familiar enough to her now not to be in any doubt how he felt. 'What has happened, *ágapitikós*, eh? What makes you so—disturbed that you are rude to my friends?'

The endearment came so easily to his lips, and Corinne brought her mind back hastily to Iole's affair. The fact that he was still seeing Persephone Chambi, whether or not she was someone else's wife, was something that would have to be gone into later. In the circumstances, she told herself, she had no need to be reticent about telling him that she had acted as Iole's go-between.

'It's—it's about Iole.'

She brushed her tongue anxiously across her lips when she saw his frown. 'Something has happened to her?' He looked tense and alert suddenly, ready to spring to his niece's rescue if need be, and Corinne felt the same thrill of tenderness for a moment that his love for the girl always inspired in her. 'She has not seen Lemou again?'

Hastily Corinne shook her head. 'No, but—she asked me to—I mean, I took a message to him for her and——'

'You did *what*?'

Gregori was on his feet and the cigarette was crushed out of existence by twisting pressure of strong fingers. Standing over her, he looked down at the top of her bowed head for several seconds, then thrust a hand under her chin and lifted her head up, forcing her to look at him—at the unmistakable anger in the set of his mouth and jaw, and the rather unexpected look of hurt in his eyes.

'Don't look at me like that, Gregori!' She got to her feet, brushing away his hand and walking over to the window to gaze unseeingly at a panorama of buildings and streets and docks below. 'I couldn't refuse to take a letter; I couldn't! Not when she was so anxious to hear about him, to know—oh, how do I know what she felt like, she didn't know she'd been let down!'

'Let down?' He had not moved and when the very stillness of him became too much to bear, she spun round and faced him again, the sun through the window making a fiery nimbus of her hair. 'Go on,' he said quietly. 'I am waiting to hear what it is that has disturbed you so much that you came here to find me.'

Corinne hesitated, her hands curling and uncurling ceaselessly. It was much harder to say, even to Gregori, than she had anticipated and she could not imagine how anyone was going to tell Iole. Gregori would do it with gentleness, she knew, and she wondered at how sure she could be of that when he had quite boldly introduced his wife to his lover only a few moments ago.

'I—I can't go back and tell her that he's flying to the United States in just a few hours,' she said huskily. 'He's leaving her, even though he knows that she's having his baby, and——'

'I would suggest it is *because* he knows!' Gregori interrupted harshly. 'What did you expect of such a man? That he would be willing to give up his freedom, his reputation as a lady-killer, to settle down to be a husband and a father?' Turning back to the desk, he took another cigarette and lit it while Corinne watched him dazedly. 'I only wish that he had gone before he caused so much damage! *Theós*, Corinne, do you expect me to weep at his departure?'

Close to tears once more, Corinne looked at him reproachfully. 'I thought you might have wept for Iole,' she told him in a small husky voice, 'she loved him!'

He drew hard on the cigarette, drawing the smoke into his lungs, then expelling it in fierce jets between his lips. 'Do you think I do not weep for her?' he demanded. 'Am I not to be the one who tells her of this—this creature's deception? Is that not why you came to see me—to ask me to break this news to her?'

Corinne caught her breath, her eyes wavering before that fiercely steady gaze. 'I—I couldn't bring myself to do it,' she confessed. 'I could have told Irine, I suppose, but I came to you. I didn't know——' She glanced at the closed door of his office, imagining him in here with Persephone Chambi, then shook her head quickly. 'I wasn't sure what you'd do about him.'

'Not even for Iole with her foolish notions of romance will I go to Takis Lemou and force him to take the responsibility of his child,' Gregori stated firmly. 'The matter will be ended when that flight to America takes off this evening, and not even you will be able to carry messages to him, even though you swore to me you did not!'

'This was the only one!'

'The crucial one, as it turns out!' Gregori said. 'And surely now you can see how right I was to forbid the association that you thought so romantic!'

Something burned inside Corinne as she looked across at him, and her hands tightened over the clasp of her bag. Ignoring the flood of tears that came pouring down her cheeks, she raged against her own hurt as fiercely as she did against Iole's. 'Oh, you're right, of course!' she whispered hoarsely. 'You're so very good at spotting a bad match, aren't you, Gregori? You slipped up badly in your own case, of course, but then you didn't want a Greek wife, did you? It would have been too—too painful for you! But you see I don't *like* being second-best, and I'm not sure how much longer I can go on accepting it! I might just decide to pack up and go home!'

He was staring at her, his fingers automatically putting out the cigarette, and she could scarcely see him for the tears that blinded her. She had shocked him, she could see that, and already she regretted having gone so far. This was not the time, not when he had to think about Iole, but she had hurt so much, seeing Persephone Chambi there with him, that she had struck out wildly.

'Corinne, what are you saying?'

'I'm saying that at this moment I wish I'd never been born,' she whispered, and moved quickly when he came towards her, evading the hands that would have reached out and taken her.

She ran from the room and on through the reception hall where the girl behind the desk stared at her in puzzled alarm. Without pause she went through the swing door and out into the street, guided by instinct rather than sight. Only as the door swung to behind her did she catch the faint sound of her name being called, and she fled from it as she did from the longings of her own heart that wanted her to go back to him.

Her sudden appearance took the chauffeur by surprise, and she had opened the door of the car and ducked inside before he could move, her voice light and breathless from running. 'Take me home!' she told him, and never for a moment gave a thought to the irony of the phrase.

CHAPTER EIGHT

IF she had given way to blind instinct when she got back from Piraeus, Corinne would have gone straight to her room without seeing anyone. But she knew that Iole would be anxiously waiting to know that her letter had been delivered, and she had to let her know, no matter what the circumstances. With any luck, Iole would be in the salon with either her mother, Zoe or Madame Kolianos, and possibly all three, so it was to the salon she went as soon as she came in.

Catching a glimpse of herself in a mirror as she passed, she was appalled to see how pale and red-eyed she looked and so obviously unhappy. Her appearance was bound to cause comment, from Madame Kolianos if from no one else, and she took a moment to try and compose herself, repairing as much damage as she could with the hasty use of make-up. Even so it was obvious that she had been crying.

She found Iole with Irine and Madame Kolianos, and managed in the first few seconds after opening the door to convey the fact that the letter had been delivered, by a nod of her head, hopefully unseen by the other two women. Iole barely inclined her head, and the look of relief in her eyes made Corinne despair of her reaction when she heard the news that Gregori had to tell her.

'Are you not coming to join us, Corinne?' Irine asked, and she shook her head.

'I just looked in to let you know I was back, that's all. I'm going up to my room.'

'Is something wrong, Corinne?' The strongly accented voice of her mother-in-law arrested her as she turned to go, and Corinne about-faced reluctantly.

'No, Mitéra.' Her answer was cautious, and it must have been obviously so, for Madame Kolianos narrowed her dark eyes shrewdly and looked at her across the room, speaking up again before she could go.

'Are you feeling unwell, *pethi*?'

In fact she felt sick with regret, but not for anything would Corinne have let that fearsome old lady know it. She had made what amounted to a threat to leave Gregori, and not waited for him to say anything in reply, but that was between her and Gregori, whatever the next move was to be. She would not discuss it with anyone else.

Unable to disguise the fact that she had been crying, Corinne nevertheless put on a brave face, and she smiled with her mouth but not her eyes. 'I'm perfectly all right, thank you, Mitéra.' But still that unrelenting voice detained her.

'You have been crying,' Madame Kolianos declared with confident certainty, 'and you look much too pale. Do you feel faint?'

'No, Mitéra, not in the least!'

Very obviously she was not believed, and Madame Kolianos was nodding her head sagely as if she knew better. 'Nevertheless you look unwell,' she insisted. 'I shall have a word with Gregori and he will see that you consult a doctor!'

Corinne knew exactly what was in her mind. It had become a regular thing lately for Madame Kolianos to enquire closely after her health, and the reason was obvious. Her mother-in-law was desperately anxious for her only son to have sons of his own to carry on the

Kolianos name, and she awaited the event with small patience. Gregori was nearly thirty-six years old and in his mother's opinion it was high time he had a family.

Normally it was something that Corinne found vaguely amusing, but not today; not as things were with her and Gregori at the moment. 'I don't need to see a doctor, Mitéra,' she insisted in a slightly unsteady voice. 'I'm not ill, I'm just very hot and tired, and I'd like to have a bath, if you'll excuse me.'

'Possibly the heat has made you pale,' Madame Kolianos conceded. 'You are not accustomed to the climate of our country yet. But mind and do not have your bath water too hot, Corinne!'

The warning followed her out of the salon, and Corinne closed the door with a sigh of relief. Having made good her escape, she hurried across the hall, keeping an anxious eye over her shoulder, just in case Iole should take it into her head to follow and ask for details about her meeting with Takis Lemou. That was the last thing she wanted to happen. At the moment she needed some time to consider her own emotional situation, not become more deeply involved in Iole's.

But she had managed to get no further than the foot of the stairs when she heard the salon door open again and footsteps coming across the hall. Iole's voice, kept low but anxious to be heard, checked her as she put a hand on the newel post. If she could have ignored the call she would have, but instead she half-turned and spoke over her shoulder.

'Please, Iole, can't it wait just a little longer, whatever it is? I don't feel like talking to anyone at the moment.'

'I wish to say that I am sorry.' Something in her voice made Corinne turn right around and face her. Iole's face was flushed and rather unhappy, and it was clear that she found it hard to say whatever it was in her mind. 'I should not have asked you to visit the *cafénion* to find Takis,' she went on, not looking at her when she spoke, 'but I had to let Takis know that I was well. You understand?'

Corinne understood all too well how hard it was going to be for Iole to accept that Takis Lemou, her precious lover, did not care how she was. She loved him with all the passion her seventeen-year-old heart was capable of, and she looked so very vulnerable standing there that Corinne felt a lump in her throat.

'I understand, Iole,' she assured her softly, 'but you don't have to blame yourself for anything. I've had a wretched morning; I shouldn't have gone in to see Gregori and I shouldn't have quarrelled with him.'

She stopped there when she saw the look in Iole's eyes and realised what she had said. 'You told him!' Iole accused, and her dark eyes were bright with anger as well as tears of reproach. 'You told Thíos Gregori, and you gave me your promise!'

'Iole, I *had* to tell him! I—I couldn't do anything else, I——' She was shaking her head, seeing herself on the brink of the very situation she had sought to avoid, and it was almost as if he came in on cue when Gregori arrived just at that moment. She had not even heard his car draw up outside, and yet there he was suddenly, and she could not pretend to be other than relieved to see him.

She forgot her own situation for a moment in her relief, watching as he came into the hall and saw her standing there with Iole. Then Iole turned quickly and went running across to him, clasping her arms tightly about him and burying her face between the open fronts of his jacket. It was an impulsive, childish gesture that must have happened a thousand times before, only this time was more than a simple homecoming.

Gregori murmured something softly in Greek, then dropped a kiss on the top of her dark head, pressing her close to his breast for a moment with one big hand at the nape of her neck; already protecting her from the hurt he knew was to come. But although his arm curved protectively around Iole's shoulders, his gaze was on Corinne at the foot of the stairs.

'Go and wait for me in the salon, *moro*,' he told Iole, and gently disengaged her arms from his waist. 'I will come and see you in just a moment, I promise. Corinne!'

She had so nearly made her escape, but Gregori's voice halted her at once, and he came striding across the hall to her, putting a restraining hand over hers on the balustrade. Corinne's heart thudded hard, and she would have given anything to avoid this moment, for she already felt too emotionally drained to face another scene with Gregori, and he obviously had something of the sort in mind.

'We must talk, Corinne.' It was almost a shock to realise that he was far more anxious than angry now, and she felt a flutter of response from her senses as the strong fingers closed over hers. 'You surely owe me an explanation after the way you left me,' he said, and Corinne looked at him dazedly for a moment.

She owed him! He seemed to mean what he said and yet she could not for the life of her imagine how he could believe it. 'You can't mean that,' she said in a quavering voice, but Gregori was frowning.

'Most certainly I do!'

'After you——' She shook her head, glancing across at the salon door. This was neither the time nor the place to settle their differences, when Iole was waiting for him; and surely in the uneasy knowledge that something had happened to bring her uncle home so unexpectedly. 'Hadn't you better go and see Iole?' she reminded him. 'She must know something is wrong, seeing you home at this time of day, when she knows I came to the office to see you.'

'You have already told her about Lemou?'

Corinne shook her head. 'No, but I let slip that I'd been to see you at the office this morning and she guessed I'd told you about her letter. She must know you'll have something to say to her, but the fact that you're here, at this time of the day——'

'Did you also tell her of your own behaviour?' he asked, and his hand squeezed hers tightly, the deep darkness of his eyes disconcertingly steady. 'Did you tell her how you ran from me in a childish tantrum and without explanation? *I* would like to hear your explanation of that incident! In fact I shall expect to do so very soon!' He glanced over his shoulder at the closed door of the salon, then turned his frown on her once more. 'I shall want to see you when I have talked with Iole and Irine,' he warned her.

'Oh *no*, Gregori!'

He narrowed his eyes and his mouth was set firm. 'I think it is necessary that we talk,' he said, and his voice was well under control as always, only his eyes showing the depth of emotion that burned in him.

'I don't want to talk!'

Her protest was instinctive, born of the fear that she might learn more about Persephone Chambi than she was able to cope with at the moment. She could not bear to hear Gregori explain the Greek woman's place in his life, as Zoe had explained it to her. It would be the last straw if she heard it from his own lips.

'I just—want to be on my own for a while to think.'

Corinne dared not look at him. Instead she kept her eyes downcast, although the intensity of his gaze did not make it easy. 'Very well,' he said after a moment or two, and his voice was hard and chill as steel. 'You shall *be* alone! I wish you joy of your solitude!'

He murmured something in his own tongue, then turned abruptly and left her, a tall angry figure that became more blurred as he went further away, because the tears in her eyes blinded her. When the door had closed behind him with studied quietness, she turned and went upstairs, but she had never felt more unhappy in her life. It would hurt less if she could hate instead of loving him so much.

Gregori had driven back to the office without coming to see her; as he had promised, he allowed her the solitude she asked for. Nor did he stay to have lunch with the family, but drove back to the office as soon as he had broken the news about Takis Lemou.

By the time Corinne eventually came downstairs, Iole had been put to bed with a sedative, and Madame Kolianos was presiding over a lunch table that was much less animated than usual. Irine was with her daughter, and from the red-rimmed look of Zoe's eyes there was little doubt that Gregori had made her see just what kind of a tragic situation she had contributed to by acting as courier for her young niece, no matter what her motives.

'You and Gregori have quarrelled about this man Lemou?' Madame Kolianos asked, quite suddenly, and took Corinne by surprise. In any case, she was given no time to answer, for her mother-in-law carried on stating her own opinion. 'You are a fool, *kopéla*! You risk your marriage to further the sordid affair of my silly little granddaughter, and wonder why Gregori is angry with you! Have you no more sense?'

'Apparently not, *madame*!' The tone of her reply brought a flush to Madame Kolianos's brown cheeks and Corinne immediately regretted her impulsiveness. She had no desire to alienate her mother-in-law, in fact she felt the need of that strong personality on her side at present. 'I'm sorry, Mitéra——' She gestured helplessly with one hand as she pushed her half-finished meal away from her. 'I'm not really hungry. If you'll excuse me I'll go——'

'You will stay and listen to the advice of an old woman if you are wise, *pethi mou*,' Madame Kolianos told her firmly. 'An old woman who does not wish to see her son's marriage break up over a matter that is now over and done with. I do not know how seriously you have quarrelled, I do not wish to know, but my advice to you, *pethi*, is to put the matter away from you, whatever it is, and do not mention it ever again!'

Corinne felt herself close to tears again and she did not want to let this strong but kindly woman see her weep if she could help it. Shaking her head, she kept her eyes downcast. 'It isn't as easy as you make it sound, Mitéra,' she said. 'It isn't just about Iole, it's—it's something more personal.'

The shrewd dark eyes narrowed slightly and from the way she was nodding her head it might almost be supposed that Madame Kolianos knew exactly what was the cause of her quarrel with Gregori. 'No matter what the cause,' she declared firmly, 'it cannot be of more importance than your marriage, Corinne. You have married a man whom you love, have you not?' Corinne nodded, for she could not deny that. 'Then you should do all you can to stay married to him, *pethí*!'

'I want to, Mitéra.'

Madame Kolianos nodded wisely. 'You have a saying, have you not? Kiss and make up, eh?' Corinne nodded, her eyes bright with unshed tears. 'Then do it, Corinne! No matter what it is between you and Gregori that is making you both so unhappy—kiss and make up! And brush the tears from your eyes, for I cannot stand the sight of weeping!' A brief dry smile was accompanied by the gentle pressure of one thin hand over hers. 'It softens my heart, and I cannot allow that!'

'Oh, Mitéra!' Such advice, and coming from that particular quarter, was at once unexpected and in one way a triumph, for she had long hoped to establish an understanding with her formidable mother-in-law.

'Now, now!' The thin fingers patted her hand reassuringly. 'If you do not eat you will be ill, and we do not wish the house to become a hospital! So eat, *pethí*, and let us have no more weeping! When your husband returns to you this evening, you forget your silly quarrelling and kiss and make up. Get me a fine grandson—that will give you something to keep you busy instead of meddling in the affairs of others!'

Corinne did not answer, but nor did she eat much more of her meal, though she made a pretence of doing so. The fact that she had at last established a rapport with her mother-in-law was something she rejoiced in, but whether or not she would be able to put Persephone Chambi far enough to the back of her mind was another matter, and she instinctively looked across at Zoe.

She had had proof enough of her sister-in-law's deviousness in Iole's case, and she might have taken consolation from that, if only the proof of Gregori's secret love had not been so sharply brought home to her that morning. It was much harder to put that meeting out of her mind than Iole's sad little romance.

When Gregori came home that evening, Corinne found it much less easy to kiss and make up than his mother suggested, for one thing because she had seldom seen him in a more aloof mood. He had some work he wished to do after dinner and he stayed in the smaller salon at the back of the house the whole evening, making no attempt to join them.

It was there Corinne found him after everyone else had gone to bed. She wanted to make up their quarrel, and she realised just how much she longed to feel his arms about her when she looked at him sitting in the light of a solitary lamp, poring over his papers. She would forgive him anything rather than risk her marriage, as Madame Kolianos had suggested she was doing, even though she had threatened in a moment of madness to leave him.

'I'm going to bed,' she ventured, and he looked up at her with dark unfathomable eyes.

Then he nodded briefly and gave his attention to what he was doing, leaving Corinne staring at him uncertainly. When he continued to ignore her she rolled her hands tightly and ran the tip of her tongue over dry lips. Her heart was hammering urgently, almost in panic.

'I'll see you later?'

Once more he glanced up briefly. 'Of course,' he said, and Corinne turned swiftly and left him, walking on legs that felt barely able to support her. She could not face the idea of his *not* coming.

It was a lot later when he came, and while Corinne heaved a sigh of relief, she could not help wondering if he had waited until he assumed she would be asleep. In-

stead she lay there in the soft lamplight with her auburn
hair spread on the pillows, shining and soft as silk, looking alluringly feminine in the pale blue silk nightgown
she had worn on her honeymoon. Chosen tonight with
deliberate intent.

The moment Gregori opened the door she felt a strange
sense of shyness, as if he was seeing her so for the first
time. She wondered what he would do and say if he
realised how long and hard she had fought the memory
of Persephone's dark beauty before she staged this moment of conciliation, or how unsure she was whether or
not he wished it. But the moment she saw the quick
gleaming desire in his eyes when he caught sight of her
from the doorway, she knew he wanted her as much as he
had ever done, regardless of his feelings for Persephone.

'I did not expect to find you still awake,' he said, and
concealed the look in his eyes with his lashes, while he
closed the door behind him. 'Can you not sleep?'

Even across the width of the room Corinne could feel
the tension in him and she raised herself on to one elbow,
watching him while he undid his shirt cuffs. 'I waited
for you,' she confessed, and detected the slightest of
pauses in the movement of those long fingers. 'Have you
been in to see how Iole is?'

He nodded briefly. 'She is being very brave, and I believe Costas will do a great deal towards a rapid recovery.
She is very young and she had an affection for Costas
once.'

'Costas?' She stared at him uncertainly for a moment,
trying not to see this as another attempt on his part to
bring about the marriage he had always wanted for his
niece. 'Does she want to see Costas?'

Gregori made no more pretence for the moment of
doing other than talk about Iole. But he stayed where he

was at the foot of the bed, his dark face illuminated by the soft light from the bedside lamp that etched it with intriguing shadows about the eyes and mouth and gave it a certain look of sadness. 'Irine agreed that it would be a good thing for her to see him,' he said. 'But before I could telephone him, he rang us, to *ask* if he could come and see her.' His mouth twisted for a moment into a bitter smile. 'The news had already reached him that Lemou had deserted her and he hoped she would need him.'

'She will need all her friends,' Corinne said. 'All the love anyone can give her in the next few months and afterwards.'

'Costas will be understanding and gentle with her because he loves her so much,' said Gregori. 'And she needs to know that she is loved by someone other than her own family.'

His gentleness when he spoke of Iole touched Corinne's heart, and she looked at him with a warmth in her eyes that she was as yet unaware of. She knew how Costas Menelus felt, for she compared their two situations. Costas had the same love for Iole as Corinne did for Gregori and both were going to have to settle for being second best if they were going to keep their loves. The only advantage Costas had was that Takis Lemou was far away in another country, while Persephone Chambi still remained to haunt her.

For a few seconds it almost weakened her resolve, but remembering that look she had seen in Gregori's eyes when he came in and saw her renewed her hopes. She was his wife, not Persephone, and in that fact lay whatever strength she possessed. 'Will Costas be allowed to see her again?' she asked, returning somewhat unwillingly to Iole for the moment. 'I understood that his father was unlikely to allow it.'

'His father is not pleased,' Gregori admitted, and by his tone suggested that Stefan Menelus had stated his opinion in no uncertain terms to Gregori himself. 'But Costas himself had no hesitation in deciding that he wished to be with Iole, even though she is having Lemou's child. And he is someone she is—comfortable with. Someone she can turn to, even though she does not love him.'

'Yes, I can understand that.'

Gregori sought and held her gaze. 'But it was not to talk about Iole that you waited for me to come, was it, Corinne?' He still did not move from the foot of the bed, and she trembled with her need for him, shaking her head slowly from side to side. 'Do you find it so difficult to talk to your husband?' he asked.

'I do when you keep your distance like that!' Corinne was stung to retort, and flushed when she detected a faint smile.

His eyes gleamed darkly with unconcealed desire, and her heart clamoured for the feel of his arms around her, but still he did not move from his place at the end of the bed. 'You expressed a wish earlier today to be left alone, Corinne, and I have no wish to impose myself upon you if you are still of the same mind. Also you spoke this morning as if you mean to leave me,' he reminded her.

Remembering his possessive fierceness when he came to take her back forcibly from Robert's island cottage, she felt her heart beat more urgently in her breast, and her mouth had a yielding softness as she looked at him, her lips parted and not quite steady. 'Would you let me?' she asked, though she had no need to ask.

The pulsing beat in her head throbbed wildly and

every nerve in her body responded to the desire in his eyes when he looked at her lying there. Still holding her gaze, he began to undo his tie as he came towards her, throwing it on to the bed and tugging at the neck of his shirt until it opened and laid bare the strong brown throat. Put the matter away and kiss and make up, no matter what it was, Madame Kolianos had advised her, and God knew Corinne was willing enough at this moment to do as she said.

She reached up and he sat on the bed close beside her, lifting her from the pillows and holding her in his arms. 'I would let you go only if you could no longer bear to be near me,' he whispered. 'Is that what you were telling me this morning, my love? That you can no longer bear to be married to me?'

'Oh no, no!'

'Then why, my love? Why did you behave as you did; say what you did?'

Corinne determinedly put the beautiful face of Persephone Chambi out of her mind and shook her head, shaking back the thick auburn hair from her face. With one hand she reached up to run her fingers through the slightly dishevelled black hair on his brow, rumpling it into further disorder. 'I think I was a little mad,' she whispered, 'but I had a reason.'

A reason he must be fully aware of, she thought, for all he continued to look at her as if he was completely mystified. 'I want to understand you, my lark,' he told her, and touched his lips to hers, lightly and repeatedly, while he spoke. 'But there are times when I think I do not know you at all. Mama believes you are behaving strangely because you are with child,' he murmured, his long hands stroking through her hair. 'But I have told her that not only is she in too much hurry, but that I would be first to know, yes?'

Corinne's lashes made two tawny brown crescents on her cheeks, and she did not raise her eyes. 'Of course you would,' she promised, but did not add that she waited only to be more certain first. Nor did she tell him how much harder it was for her to accept the existence of his mistress now that she thought she might be having his child. Although almost certainly it would tip the balance in her favour.

'How could you think of leaving me?' He kissed her mouth lightly, moving his lips down to her neck and throat and the soft, shadowy vee of her breasts. 'Do you not love me?' he demanded in a husky whisper, and pressed her closer until the hard, virile leanness of him kindled responses she could scarcely control. 'Tell me, Corinne, my love, my lark! Why did you run away from me as you did? Why did you speak as you did?'

Her fingers running through his hair until it stood in thick curls as it always did when it was dishevelled, tightened suddenly and she pulled until he was forced to look up. 'Don't you really know?' she asked in a small unsteady voice, and he shook his head.

'I only know that I was more fearful of losing you in those few moments than I have ever been,' he confessed with a candour that completely disarmed her.

'Oh, Gregori!'

She spoke in a whisper and her hands stroked the lean brown face that hovered above her, the dark eyes deep and glowing in a way that brought a shivering need to surrender. He kissed her mouth lingeringly, his breath warm on her lips when he spoke.

'You have bewitched me, you little *magissa*!' he whispered with mock ferocity. 'I should be more firm and make you explain your behaviour this morning, but I have no wish to listen to explanations when I would so much rather love you as I know you want me to love you. You will tell me in your own time, I know—you will not be able to help yourself. I know you *that* well, *ágapitikós!*'

Corinne traced the firm straight line of his mouth with a finger-tip until he took it between his strong teeth and bit gently.

'Don't question me,' she begged in a husky whisper. 'Not now, my darling—I love you. Let's kiss and make up, hmm?'

He was smiling, drawing her back to him and holding her more tightly than ever while he buried his face in her thick hair, his voice muffled against her neck. *'Magissa!'* he repeated in a deep and huskily harsh voice. 'You are a witch, but I love you, and I need you more than you will ever know!'

He murmured in his own tongue while he sought her lips again, leaning over to press her back into the pillows, his mouth hard and urgent, kissing her as if there was a desperate hunger in him that must be satisfied. And for a while Corinne managed to forget the smooth dark beauty of Persephone Chambi and gave herself up to the wild and passionate desires that only this man could arouse in her.

The next few days were the happiest that Corinne had known for some time, for she had almost forgotten Persephone. Just occasionally something reminded her, but even then she could convince herself that it was she who had the best of the situation, for she was Gregori's wife, and he loved her. Perhaps only as Zoe had suggested 'in a way', but it was a way that Corinne could find little cause to complain of.

She was almost sure now that she was having Gregori's child and she could scarcely wait to have it confirmed so that she could tell him with certainty. As soon as she was able, she made an appointment with a doctor in Piraeus; a man who was half English and whom she had heard about through hearing Zoe mention him as a friend.

She quite often took a car and a chauffeur and went shopping on her own, so that no one questioned her about why or where she was going. Why she had chosen a part-English doctor was perhaps because she sometimes admitted to homesickness and an English doctor, even though he was only partly so, would make her feel more at ease.

Doctor Merron proved to be a charming man, although he merely smiled when she said she had heard of him through her sister-in-law. It was much too soon to be certain, he told her, which was no more than she expected, but when he had done certain tests he would be able to tell her for certain. A few days perhaps—next week.

Corinne nodded, happily convinced in her own mind, and showing as much by her expression. Looking at her for a moment as she prepared to leave, he seemed to unbend a little from the formal professional manner, and smiled at her.

'You are very certain in your own mind, are you not, Mrs Kolianos?' he asked, and Corinne laughingly admitted it as she picked up her handbag.

'I'm quite certain,' she told him. 'But I have to have your verdict before I proclaim it abroad!'

Once more the shrewd professional eyes regarded her steadily, and he nodded. 'I have learned in my years as a doctor to trust feminine intuition in these matters, Mrs Kolianos, although it is very unprofessional of me to admit it, of course. I am quite sure Gregori will be delighted.'

'Oh, do you know Gregori as well as Zoe?' Corinne was, as ever, happy to talk about her husband, and the doctor was nodding and smiling.

'Indeed I do, Mrs Kolianos; I was at your wedding.'

There was hardly need for her to apologise, for she had known very few of the people at her wedding, but she pulled a face when she made a token apology. 'I'm sorry, Doctor Merron, but there were so many people, and I was in rather a daze——'

'But of course you were,' he allowed smilingly. 'I have known the Kolianoses for a number of years, although only socially, you understand. That's how I know how pleased Gregori will be to hear that he is to become a father, although I would stress that I am not making that a definite statement until I have those tests back next week.' His dark Greek eyes smiled at her in friendly speculation as he saw her to the door. 'You will not, I suspect, wait so long to tell your husband?'

Corinne's eyes sparkled confidently, warming to his friendliness, especially when she knew he was a family friend, someone who would know just how welcome the news would be. 'I think I'll go and see Gregori before I go home,' she said. Today it was somehow easier to dismiss the memory of her last visit, when she had found Persephone Chambi on the point of leaving when she arrived. She could think only of how excited Gregori would be with her news. 'I don't make a habit of calling on him at the office,' she confided, 'but I think today could be called an exception to the rule, don't you?'

'Almost certainly,' Doctor Merron agreed, and glanced at his wristwatch. 'And he will very likely have returned to the office by now, it is more than an hour ago since I saw him.'

'Lunching out?' Corinne asked. Curious because Gregori so seldom went out to lunch. 'Oh, he was entertaining a business contact, very likely.'

'Very possibly.' Something in Doctor Merron's manner made her draw a deep breath suddenly and the rate of her pulse increased just slightly without any definable cause as yet. 'I am sure he will be delighted to see you, Mrs Kolianos.'

Corinne gripped both hands tightly over the catch of her handbag and tried to appear much more casual than she was feeling. It was not in her nature to be devious, and yet in the present situation she felt not only justified but well within her rights, even though it made her feel slightly sick as she asked the question.

'You probably know Kíria Chambi too, don't you, doctor?'

The dark eyes looked at her for a moment as if they suspected a trap, but he nodded. 'Yes,' he said quietly. 'I know Kíria Chambi also.'

'Then it was probably she who was lunching with my husband, wasn't it?'

Obviously he would much rather not have answered her, but Corinne was looking at him with a bright unwavering gaze that compelled a response. 'I believe it was, Mrs Kolianos,' he said. 'And now, if you will forgive my brusqueness, I have another appointment.'

'Yes, of course. I'm sorry to have taken up so much of your time—I know you must be busy.' Her voice sounded vague and not quite steady and Corinne felt a sudden need to be in the open air. 'Thank you, doctor—goodbye!'

She felt rather as if someone had struck her a blow

and knocked the breath out of her. All the happiness of the past few days she now saw as a fool's paradise. The fact that Gregori had been lunching with Persephone while she herself was on her way to confirm that she was having his child left a bitter taste in her mouth and she wanted to weep in anger and frustration.

'Mrs Kolianos, are you feeling quite well? Should you perhaps sit here for a while until you feel better able to——'

'No, no, really!' She dismissed the need for his professional concern hastily. 'I'm perfectly all right, doctor, thank you. The fresh air will soon clear my head.'

'If you are quite sure.'

Obviously he was far from happy to see her leaving when she was so obviously agitated, but there was little he could do to detain her if she was of a mind to leave, and eventually he shrugged resignedly and saw her out.

'I shall of course be seeing you about the results next week?' he asked, and she nodded.

'Yes, of course. Goodbye.'

She left the building hurriedly, consumed by a chaos of emotions that confused her with their complexity. Anger brought a bright hot flush to her cheeks and unhappiness gave a droop to her mouth, her eyes stinging with unshed tears as she walked without having the least idea of the direction she took at first.

Then gradually her brain began to clear and she realised how impulsively she had reacted. If Doctor Merron was not conversant with Gregori's affair, then she had almost certainly given him a strong clue; and if he was then she had shown quite clearly how she felt about it.

Nothing had changed, she told herself as she made her way back through the maze of Piraeus's streets to where she had left the car. The doctor had merely reminded her of Persephone's continuing existence in the background, that was all. He had revived the bitterness of that first encounter, aroused the furious jealousy that she had vowed she would control because she, not Persephone, had the upper hand in the long run.

She had a free choice, she decided. Either she could leave and go back home to England and never see Gregori again, or she could stay and put up with the knowledge that always in the background, like a cloud on an otherwise sunny horizon, was Persephone Chambi. The light, unconscious pressure of one hand allowed her to imagine she could already feel the pulse of the new life she carried, and she knew what she would do.

'Corinne!'

She was snatched swiftly from her reverie, and turned around at once. Robert came running after her along the narrow, shadowed street, his face red and shiny with the heat, and his sudden appearance brought a welcome sense of comfort to Corinne in her present mood, so that she greeted him eagerly.

'Robert—where did you spring from?'

'Didn't you hear me yelling at you?' he asked with a great blow of relief when he stopped running. 'Hello, darling, how are you?'

He did not hesitate but bent and kissed her mouth, an arm thrust familiarly about her waist as he fell into step with her, and she made no objection. 'I'm fine, thank you, Robert.' Her answer was absent and her mind was so obviously on other things that he frowned briefly. 'Are you still enjoying island life?'

'Not for much longer.' He dismissed the question airily, seemingly more interested in talking about her. 'You don't look fine to me,' he declared with his customary forthrightness. 'What's wrong, Corinne? Isn't it as much fun being a millionaire's wife as it ought to be? Be honest, darling; this is old faithful Robert, remember? Just say the word and if he's not treating you right I'll sort him out, no matter how much he glowers at me!'

It was such a temptation to tell him what was wrong. To pour out her troubles to him; about Gregori and Persephone, and how for a while she had managed to push the other woman into the background and revel in the love of her husband. But she loved Gregori no matter what happened, and not even to Robert could she say a word against him.

So she smiled. 'There's no need to sound so belligerent, Robert,' she told him. 'I get along with everyone very well now, except perhaps Zoe, and I have no regrets at all.' She placed a hand over the one that hugged her comfortingly close, and smiled up at him. 'But thank you for being so ready to champion me.'

'Haven't I always?' Robert demanded, and she nodded. Looking at her slightly pale face and the too bright eyes that just evaded his, he squeezed her tightly for a moment. 'Just see that you remember it. I'm glad to see you're not so wary of being seen with me, though, that at least is an improvement. Has your Greek tyrant relented?'

'I don't know.' She sounded far more offhand than she felt. 'I don't think he's likely to see us anyway, he's— busy.'

Robert looked faintly surprised at her manner, but said nothing more. 'I was going to give you a ring, as a matter of fact,' he told her. 'I'm going back tomorrow, and you promised you'd see me before I went.'

'Tomorrow?'

Taken aback, she swallowed hard, for she felt rather as if she was at the end of an era with Robert departing, and he was eyeing her as if he knew how she felt. 'If you're sorry I'm going,' he said, 'I shall probably give up my job and stay for good! Seriously though, darling, the party's over as far as I'm concerned, and I can't honestly say that Greece is much fun without you. Each time I went to the top of that hill behind the quay I thought about our picnic and how perfect it was with just you and me. Greek islands are idyllic, my sweet, only if you're in the right frame of mind, and without you I'm not.'

'Oh, Robert, I'm sorry!'

She spoke as if she was on the verge of crying and from his look Robert guessed it. Making an effort to be facetious, he cocked a brow at her, his eyes less quizzical and more anxious than he realised. 'Because I don't like your Greek islands, or because I'm going?' he teased.

'I'm just sorry that you couldn't have enjoyed your holiday more; that things couldn't have been different for you.'

'Couldn't be in the circs, darling,' he told her with forced carelessness. 'You apparently loved your Greek after all!'

Corinne caught her bottom lip between her teeth, and her eyes had a mistiness she did her best to hide. 'Yes,' she agreed huskily, 'I love my Greek.'

CHAPTER NINE

CORINNE had not been to see Gregori at the office after all. Having said goodbye to Robert she found herself in a very different mood from the happy excitement with which she had anticipated telling Gregori about the baby, and she had gone straight home.

It was not the first time that he was a little later coming home either, but the fact that he did so that evening, when she was feeling as she did, simply added to her dispirited outlook. When he immediately came across to her the moment he came in and kissed her as he always did, she almost hated him for his duplicity, even while she lifted her mouth for his kiss.

She was unusually quiet during dinner and afterwards, although the fact seemed to go unnoticed, and she did not feign sleep as she thought of doing when Gregori came to bed either. Instead she responded to his lovemaking because she could not help herself, and because no matter what he did she loved him as desperately as ever.

But it was a long time before she slept. Lying there in the dark beside him, trying to untangle her tortured emotions, her mind was alive with questions and no answers, and she was no nearer to solving anything when she eventually drifted into a restless sleep. As a result she woke later and Gregori, as he sometimes did, had not disturbed her before he left, but let her sleep on.

It was all the more surprising therefore when she eventually went downstairs herself, to find him still seated at the table with his mother and Zoe. He said little, but leaned across and kissed her cheek when she took her place beside him, and while she ate her somewhat frugal breakfast, she got the feeling that he was waiting impatiently for her to finish.

'You look tired, *pethi*,' Madame Kolianos observed. 'Are you not sleeping properly?'

Gregori appeared to notice the shadows about her eyes then, and he stroked a long hand down her cheek, pressing the backs of his fingers to her brow and smiling enquiringly at her. 'I'm all right, Mitéra,' she assured her mother-in-law. 'I just took a long time going off last night, that's all.'

'Ah!' The conclusion she came to was so obvious that Corinne felt herself colouring under the gaze of those shrewd dark eyes. 'You should take care and get plenty of sleep,' Madame Kolianos counselled. 'We cannot have you so pale and tired in the mornings.'

'No, Mitéra.'

She reached for a second bread roll and began buttering it, conscious of Gregori watching her, so that she found it hard not to look at him. Leaning an elbow on the table he watched her eat, uncaring that he obviously made her self-conscious.

'I hope you are not too tired, my love,' he said. 'I am taking you for a drive this morning.' Corinne, taken by surprise, simply stared at him uncomprehendingly for a moment, not knowing quite how to react.

Her pulse was fluttering uneasily as she tried to think of a reason for this unprecedented departure from the normal, and she was too wary to do anything more than murmur acceptance, and a brief, irresistible question. 'To anywhere special?' she asked, and Gregori's dark eyes sought and held hers steadily for a second or two before he replied. A response that betrayed his impatience by the tone of his voice.

'*Yes*, my love!'

Madame Kolianos glanced from one to the other and Corinne, noticing her tight-lipped look, hoped her mother-in-law was not going to remark on his abruptness, however well-intentioned she might be. In the event the old lady said nothing, and the moment Corinne had finished her meal Gregori got up from the table and reached for her hand, offering that brief but irresistible invitation she was so accustomed to.

'Hmm?'

Obediently she placed her hand in his, but she felt much too unsure of him for her own peace of mind. He could always persuade her, coax her back to him, no matter how resolutely she tried to harden her heart. And when she considered the choice she had, of years ahead when she must suffer the presence of Persephone Chambi always there in the background, or of giving up Gregori altogether and taking herself and their unborn child back to England, she knew she would always follow her heart.

When she came down, ready to go, she found him waiting in the hall for her, and he took her hand again, holding it tightly and pressing it with his own to the spot where his heart thudded strongly in his breast. Instead of making for the main garden where it was possible to get lost among the shrubs and trees, they went around the side of the house to where a small forecourt fronted the garages, and was itself surrounded by garden on three sides.

'Aren't you going to the office this morning?' she asked, unable to contain her curiosity.

She had not meant to sound so flatly discouraging and only realised it when she saw his expression, one black brow slightly arched. It was simply that he so seldom took time off from his work that when it happened she knew inevitably that it was with very good reason; and it was the nature of his reason in this instance that made her so uneasy.

'You wish to be rid of me?' Gregori enquired, soft-voiced, and she hastened to deny it.

'No,' she said in a small voice. 'No, of course I don't want to be rid of you.'

'I am very relieved to hear it!'

She allowed him the mild sarcasm without reproach, because she was so very unsure of herself, but she still eyed him warily, and they were out of sight of the house when Gregori brought them to a standstill suddenly. Putting his hands on her shoulders he turned her to face him, and Corinne noticed in a brief upward glance how disturbingly dark and fathomless his eyes looked.

'So quiet and distant,' he said, and Corinne stirred uneasily. 'You have seen Robert.'

Taken by surprise, she looked up quickly, but he appeared so calm that it was almost alarming, and her heart thudded hard and urgently. Perhaps he no longer cared whether or not she saw Robert; perhaps it was part of what he had planned for her. To let her know that he would go his way and she was free to go hers, although if she had stopped to think clearly, she would have known that was not it.

As it was her eyes had a bright, hurt look that shimmered with unshed tears when she admitted to having seen Robert again. 'Yes, I've seen him,' she said huskily, then added with a bitterness she was unaware of, 'How do you know?'

'I saw you.'

Corinne was trembling and she hoped he was not aware

of it, even though he still had his hands on her shoulders. 'When you were coming back from lunch, no doubt?' she guessed, and his acceptance of the jibe added to her fears, so that she went on without stopping to think. 'You're surely not going to have the nerve to object, are you? You can hardly act the injured innocent in the circumstances, can you? Sauce for the goose is sauce for the gander, you know!'

The fact that he said nothing for several seconds was startling in itself, but that he seemed puzzled rather than angry was both unexpected and disturbing, and she found his steady, slightly frowning gaze unnerving. 'You seem to think that the adage applies in some way to me,' he said, and Corinne caught her breath.

If only she did not feel such an overwhelming need to lay her head on his breast and feel the comfort of his arms around her! Instead she stood there with his hands on her shoulders, his strong fingers digging deeply into her flesh and stunningly aware of the lean, virile body that was just a breath away, and the hands that seemed to be trying to restrain her, even though she had made no move as yet to walk away from him.

'I was saying goodbye to Robert,' she told him without attempting to explain her earlier statement. 'He—he's gone home.'

'Thank God!'

Quickly reproachful, Corinne blinked back her tears. 'I shall miss him, whatever you feel about it,' she told him. 'Even though I haven't been able to see him since I was married, thanks to your ban.'

'I thank God that he has gone back to England,' Gregori said, 'because now that he is gone I can relax a little.' He noticed her frown and smiled faintly. 'I had the fear constantly in my mind that you would one day dis-

appear and go back with him,' he confessed. 'And I could
not have let you go, my lark.'

Thinking of Persephone, and how she was expected to
turn a blind eye to his affair with her, Corinne was suddenly angry, and her cheeks were flushed as she looked
up at him. 'Oh, why do you have to be so—so two-
faced?' she demanded huskily, and pulled herself free
of his hands. 'I almost envy Iole sometimes! At least
Takis Lemou had the honesty to discard her instead of
marrying her and playing out a—a role, and pretending
to love her! Do you imagine it's any less hurtful because
you're more subtle, Gregori?'

The warning light was in Gregori's dark eyes, but he
also looked genuinely confused by her words, and she
found that hard to take. 'I do not understand you,' he
said. 'What have Iole and Lemou to do with you and
me, Corinne?'

Her face streaked with big rolling tears, Corinne
looked up at him in despair. 'Oh, don't go on with it,
Gregori! Don't pretend you don't know what I'm talking about—you know well enough how often you see
your—your friend! And I wish I could hate you for it.'
Her tangled emotions took over from common sense,
and she spoke much too quickly and without thought,
her voice catching every so often in a breathless sob in her
throat. 'I know about Persephone Chambi; I know you
deceived me, that you've gone on deceiving me ever since
we were married! I know you don't love me as you do
her, Zoe told me and I've tried not to care, but I do! I
do care!'

'Oh, Corinne!' He moved swiftly, taking her tear-
stained face gently between his big hands, then he bent
to kiss her lips. 'As *I* care, *ágapitikós*! I have never deceived you in any but this one thing, and God knows it

was never meant to hurt you—quite the opposite, as you shall soon see.'

It would be unbearable to hear it from his own lips, and Corinne as she stared up at him felt herself go cold suddenly, so that she shivered. She did not want to hear how he loved Persephone Chambi in a way he could never love her; that he had deceived her because he did not want to hurt her. She would rather go on living in her fool's paradise than hear it from him as she had from Zoe.

'No,' she whispered. 'Don't tell me, please, I don't want to hear it!'

'Corinne, my love, my lark!'

Her drew her into his arms and held her tightly, his face buried in the rich auburn hair that muffled the soft words he spoke in his own tongue. And Corinne clung to him in a desperate attempt to shut out everything but the comfort of his nearness, and the precious endearments that he murmured against her ear.

Inevitably she was soothed by the softness of that deep voice and the gentleness of his hands, his lips on her neck and her cheeks, kissing the tears from her eyes until she eventually leaned against him too bemused to realise that she had yielded yet again to that irresistible magic he wove for her.

He eased her away from him, his hands cradling her head while he looked down into her eyes that were red with weeping. Then he kissed the corner of her mouth. 'Do you trust me enough to drive with me?' he asked, and stroked the dishevelled hair from her brow with a light caressing finger. 'I promise that you shall know just how much I love you; how little desire I had to hurt you. Nor will you have reason to hate me as you have been trying so hard to do. Oh, I know you have,' he in-

sisted as he put a hand beneath her chin to bring her
mouth up to him. His lips were lingeringly gentle and at
the same time ardent enough to bring a response from
her, and his dark eyes gleamed fervently as he looked
down at her. 'Will you come with me, my lark?' he asked.

Through her tears Corinne looked at the dark face,
at once tender and passionate, and she could find no
other response in her but to nod agreement. Drawing her
close again he kissed her more fiercely, holding her so
tightly that she felt her own body fused with the virile
strength of his, and despite her tears, she clung to him
desperately.

'I'll come with you,' she whispered.

They had driven several kilometres along the lovely pine-
bordered coast road under the shadow of Mount Hymettus, and Corinne began to feel a stirring of excitement
that she could not account for. She could not even begin
to guess what Gregori had in store for her, but her heart
urged her to trust him, that he did not mean her any
hurt, and she gradually became more alert to the route
they were taking as they drove along.

There were houses built among the trees; huge villas
that gleamed whitely amid the dark, scented pines and
red rock, and Corinne glanced at him quickly from the
corner of her eye when Gregori turned into a narrow
road, very similar to the one that gave access to the
Kolianos home. The house appeared to be slightly larger
but of very similar design, and it sat, benignly inviting, in
the hot summer sunshine.

Corinne's heart began to beat more urgently as they
drove right round in front of the double doors that stood
in shade below an overhanging upper storey. The garden
here was as big too, but a little less formal, and hibiscus,

oleander and every other conceivable tree and shrub bloomed in riotous profusion right to the very walls of the house.

There was a warmth about the place, an air of peace, and yet it seemed to suggest emptiness, and she gazed at it curiously while Gregori came round to help her from the car. Holding her arm, he stood and gazed with her at the rambling white house with its big wooden doors still firmly closed, then he bent his head slightly to speak close to her ear.

'Does it please you, my lark?' he asked softly, and Corinne stared at him for a moment. His eyes gleamed darkly and a white smile beamed in the dark face. 'It is ours, *ágapiménos*, I hope you like my choice of a home for us. It has few furnishings as yet, but we can choose them at our leisure, it is comfortable enough for the moment and lacks none of the essentials.'

'Oh, Gregori!'

Her voice was a bare whisper of sound, and she felt tears in her eyes once more, though they were tears of happiness now. It was such a different kind of revelation from what she expected and she looked from the big house to his face in happy bewilderment. With an arm about her waist and obviously well pleased with her reaction, Gregori took her under the shadowy balcony to the front doors and ushered her in ahead of him— watching, waiting with an anxiety that sat strangely on him.

The walls were bare of decoration, but they gleamed whitely and were barred and patterned with sunlight from a tall window, and there were rugs on the tiled floor, carpet softening the marble treads of the wide staircase. It was beautiful and Corinne loved it, immediately and unreservedly, because he had bought it for her. She could see it as their home; her and Gregori and the baby she carried, and she placed a hand quite unconsciously over the place where she felt so sure a new life was growing.

'Well, my love?'

Gregori's voice, soft and enquiring and vaguely anxious, brought her back to reality, and she turned to him with her eyes still hazy with the dreams she had been making, shining with a look of love that gave them a brightness and beauty they had never had before.

'It's perfect,' she whispered. 'It's quite beautiful.'

'As you are, my love.' He turned her into his arms and held her tightly, his dark eyes deep and gleaming and watching her mouth with the look of a man who knows a desperate hunger. He kissed her with such fervour that when he eventually let her go she clung to him breathlessly. 'You will be happier in our own home, eh?' he asked, and kissed her once more before she could admit it. 'Oh, my lark, I have so longed to have you to myself, to find you here alone when I come back in the evenings; not to have to wait to love you until we can be alone!'

The shade of Persephone stirred uneasily in the back of Corinne's mind for a moment, but she fought it back determinedly, lifting her mouth to his kiss once more. 'I love you,' she whispered. 'Perhaps more than you'll ever know.'

His hands stroked and caressed her soft skin and she pressed closer to him, willing this moment to go on forever. 'I *shall* know, my love,' he murmured, his lips against her neck. 'You will show me how much you love me, *ágapiménos*, you will see.' He kissed her mouth hard, then raised his head and looked down at her, an expression on his face that brought a momentary flutter of anxiety to her heart. 'But alas, not at this moment.'

Corinne eased herself away from him, just far enough to see his face, and he bent and kissed her brow. 'The former owner is coming to see us, my sweetheart, to wish us well, and to assure herself that you like our new home.'

'*Her*self?' A small cold finger of doubt traced its way shiveringly along Corinne's spine, but there was no time for explanations, for she could hear another car outside and she felt a fleeting moment of sheer panic as she looked up at him. 'Gregori?'

Persephone Chambi came into the hall after a preliminary tap on the door. Tall and elegant, she was smiling and obviously very happy, so that it was hard for Corinne to think logically as she watched her approach. When she was half way across the mosaic-tiled hall, she turned and called over her shoulder, something in Greek.

A child came in, a little boy about eight years old, and close on his heels a man of middle height and slightly corpulent, with thick black hair going grey and a smile as wide and open and Persephone's. 'We all came,' Persephone said as she took the child's hand in hers. 'I hope you do not mind, Kiría Kolianos?'

Too dazed to say anything and no longer sure that she was quite certain of her sanity, Corinne said nothing but merely shook her head, leaving Gregori to answer for her. He had an arm about her and she found his nearness reassuring as she listened to him welcome the newcomers, smiling at all three with equal pleasure.

'Of course we are delighted, Persephone,' he told her, and proffered his hand to the man. 'Heracles, it is good to see you again, my friend! Such a pity you could not have been at our wedding, eh?'

Broad shoulders shrugged resignedly, lips pursed. 'A business trip,' the man said. 'And Persephone had arranged to come with me. You should not do these things in such haste, eh, my friend?'

Gregori's smile appreciated his laughter, and he looked down at the little boy standing beside his mother. 'And Miklos!' He shook the child's hand, speaking to him in Greek for a moment, and Corinne realised a little dazedly as she listened to him that he was giving her time to recover her composure. 'Corinne, *ágapitikós*,' he said after a moment or two, 'you have already met Persephone; this is her husband, Heracles Chambi, and her son, Miklos. My wife.'

He said the last with such unmistakable pride that Corinne's heart hammered wildly in her breast as she shook hands, murmuring polite greetings. She knew from Persephone's expression that she realised at last the reason for her behaviour at their last meeting, and colour flooded into Corinne's cheeks. But at the same time she felt as if a great weight had been lifted from her, and as she stood with Gregori's arm about her, she felt suddenly and for the first time that she was really his wife.

'You like your house?' Persephone asked, and her eyes had the same friendly warmth that Corinne had noticed and resented the first time they met.

'I love it,' she assured her. 'Kiría Chambi——'

'Persephone,' the gentle voice corrected her, and Persephone smiled. 'I have been friends with the Kolianos family for a very long time, and I would like to think that we could be friends also.'

Corinne swallowed hard, thankful that Gregori was for the moment engaged in conversation with Heracles Chambi. 'I'd like that,' she said. 'Thank you, Persephone.'

Persephone's dark eyes looked at the tell-tale signs of weeping and she shook her head. 'It is a wonderful thing to be a cherished wife,' she said. 'I know you will like the house because Gregori bought it for you with love in his heart.'

'It was yours?'

Persephone nodded. 'My father left it to me in his will, but I have little use for it.' She smiled at her husband in a way there was no disguising. 'I too am a cherished wife, Corinne, and my husband provides the home I need. Gregori was so sure that you would like this one that he offered to buy it from me.'

Holding tightly to her pride, Corinne looked at her steadily. 'It was to do with the house that you came to the office that day, of course,' she said, and Persephone put a hand on her arm.

'Of course. These things take so long and require so much complicated dealing that we had to meet several times, although I tried not to intrude upon his working hours too often. But he was so afraid that you would discover his secret and spoil the surprise.'

'Oh, if only I *had* known!'

Persephone smiled understandingly and once more pressed a hand over her arm reassuringly. 'You realise now, eh?' she asked, and Corinne nodded. 'So, now that I know you are going to be happy in your new home,' Persephone said, 'we will leave you to enjoy it. *Kaló ríziko!*'

It was in something of a daze that Corinne watched them depart, and as their car disappeared along the narrow little road that cut them off from the main highway, she turned back to find Gregori immediately behind her. His hands on her arms, he turned her to face him and, knowing now how she had misjudged him, she kept her eyes downcast.

'I'm sorry.' Her voice was small and barely audible, and she caught her breath when Gregori put a hand under her chin.

'Because you suspected me of having an affair with Persephone?' he asked, and laughed as he bent to kiss her mouth. 'I had no idea that you thought me an adulterer, my lark,' he told her with mock severity, 'or I might have treated you less gently!'

'I thought——' She hesitated because her heart was thudding with breathtaking urgency and she had a wild longing to be in his arms, to erase the suspicion and anger she seemed to have harboured for so long. 'Zoe told me that you wanted to marry Persephone and that you still loved her. I—I hated her, at least——'

'You tried to hate me too,' Gregori reminded her, 'but you are not made for hate, my lark, you are made for love; *my* love.' His dark eyes speculated for a moment on her response before he went on. 'I do not deny that had Persephone been free when we first met, I might have had an affair with her, she is a very beautiful woman and I have always been susceptible to beautiful women. But I have never had the slightest desire to marry her, not even if she had not been so devoted to her Heracles.'

Ready and willing to believe him, Corinne was nevertheless puzzled by Zoe's attitude. 'Then why did Zoe——'

'Zoe what you call—hero-worshipped?—Persephone when she was much younger,' he told her with a wry smile, 'and she has never really grown out of it. Also, of course, she was trying to make me pay for stopping Iole's affair with Takis Lemou; my sister is passionately devoted to our niece. She resented my marrying anyone but Persephone and obviously invented some story about my undying love for her. But not even for my beloved but over-spoiled sister would I marry a woman I did not love.'

'And I believed her!'

'And you believed her,' Gregori echoed softly, and lifted her face with a hand under her chin, his eyes searching her face for a hint of a smile. 'My brother Dimitri married the woman he loved,' he told her, 'and I vowed to do the same, even though my father once found a bride for me and meant me to marry her.'

Corinne remembered how evasive Irine had been when she questioned her about Gregori ever having been close to marriage before, and she looked up at him. 'I spoke to Irine about you having been near to getting married before,' she confessed, 'and she neither denied nor confirmed it. I thought she knew about Persephone too.'

'Oh, my love, how foolish you are!' He pressed her close and his lips brushed her neck while he talked. 'I have never wanted any woman for my wife other than the one I am married to—will you believe that?'

'I believe it,' Corinne whispered, and lifted her mouth to him.

He kissed her with a gentleness she found even more exciting than his fierceness, because it promised the passion she knew he was capable of, and his lips lingered on the eager softness of her mouth. 'And that son you carry will be as handsome as even Mama could wish for,' he murmured when he gave her freedom to draw breath for a moment, 'eh, my lark?'

Corinne looked up at him with starry eyes, and she could have sworn that the child stirred within her. 'You know?'

'Am I wrong?' Gregori challenged, and she did not stop to think about Doctor Merron's official confirmation, for even he had admitted to trusting a woman's intuition.

'I'm almost sure,' she told him, and Gregori drew her once more into the fiercely possessive circle of his arms, then bent and slid an arm under her legs, lifting her off her feet and cradling her against his chest.

'I have furnished the bedroom,' he told her with a gleam in his dark eyes that sent tiny thrills along her spine. 'A bridal suite, my love, for this is where our marriage really begins! The rest of the house will be furnished in time, but this was the most important; and just in case you should ever doubt my love for you again——'

'I never shall,' Corinne promised, and clung to him tightly as he carried her up the wide, steep staircase of their new home. 'But please convince me.'

Complete and mail this coupon today!